by
Sam Godwin
and illustrated by Joanna Roberts

HENDERSON
PUBLISHING PLC
©1996 HENDERSON PUBLISHING PLC

PART 1

1813

i

The Ancient One lay in his coffin, his eyes bulging with hatred, his limbs bound tightly with cord. The fools were dancing in a circle around him, throwing wood and bales of straw on the pyre underneath him. He wanted to rise and destroy them, cutting a swathe through them like a sickle felling corn. But they had placed a silver crucifix on the coffin. He wasn't afraid of the cross but the silver was another matter. It sent his mind reeling. One touch and it burnt his flesh, like acid on human skin.

The fools stopped dancing and began praying. Didn't the idiots know that he was invincible, that he had gone through a thousand such deaths and mutilations only to rise again triumphant after a few nights? Let them have their fun, he decided. They shall pay dearly for their indiscretions.

The fools' leader, an old priest who walked with the aid of a cane, sprinkled him with holy water. It fizzled on the wood and the Ancient One roared. The noise drew gasps from the fools. "Burn him now, for goodness' sake," someone cried. "Destroy the evil one before the sun sets completely and he turns more of us into living corpses."

The priest lit a taper and held it high above his head. "Let him who invaded our beloved village of Ari Lasov be gone," he chanted. "Let him depart with all his pain and darkness."

Imbeciles, thought the Ancient One. There is no place on earth that can be rid of me. I shall be here long after your bones have turned to dust. My kind shall rule this village and all that live within it.

The priest held the taper to the wood. There was a crackle as the first twigs caught fire. The Ancient One steeled himself against the coming pain. It will be over soon, he told himself. It is not the end. Soon he was engulfed in roaring flames. The sun was gone now, its weak light extinguished by the autumn night. But it was too late for the Ancient One to escape. Begrudgingly he released his spirit, letting it flutter above the trees like a lost bird.

I am indestructible, was his last thought. I will be back.

ii

The girl and the monk slipped out of Ari Lasov shortly before midnight. They travelled down the mountain in a horse drawn coach, the girl huddled in the dark behind thick curtains, the monk sitting next to the driver. They reached the mountain valley by dawn, where the girl was forced to seek shelter in a farm on account of her condition.

When the moon rose that night, they resumed their journey, reaching the harbour in the small hours of the morning. The girl was smuggled on board a merchant ship inside a coffin, brought to the harbour by members of the monk's order. She drank nothing during the journey, except the blood of flies that wandered into her coffin.

In Shanghai, the coffin was lowered on to the docks and carried into a disused warehouse. The girl came out, tired but uncomplaining.

"We are waiting for another coach," said the monk. He spoke to her as little as possible, from the other side of the enormous room. She nodded but said nothing. She had discovered that she could communicate with mortals by sending messages to their minds. Not that she had anything to say to the monk. He was a prejudiced fool. He considered her to be evil. And like the people of Ari Lasov he blamed her for what had happened.

The coach arrived in the evening, driven by a young Tibetan novice who had accepted the Christian faith. The girl liked his round face, his enormous, kind eyes. She climbed inside the coach to make sure the windows were sealed against the light. Satisfied, she settled on the hard, wooden seat. It was raining heavily, so the monk got in beside her. During the journey, he feasted on honey, bread and dried fruit. The girl did not eat. She did not need to, and she wasn't hungry.

Between meals, the monk mumbled long, tedious prayers in Latin, one hand closed around a necklace of garlic bulbs about his neck. The girl found it hard not to laugh. The garlic did not scare her in the least. On the contrary, its powerful scent reminded her of better times, of long suppers around the fire at home.

His praying was piercingly loud in her ears, for her sense of hearing had become as sharp as that of a bat. She screwed up her face and stuck her fingers into her ears, in an attempt to deaden the noise.

Three days later the coach stopped at the foot of Mount Everest. It was night, and a full moon was shining on the bare rocks.

"Get out," said the monk to the girl. "We have to use mules from now on. The mountain is too steep for a horse drawn coach."

She obeyed without question. The young Tibetan novice brought them mules and they resumed their journey at once. At sunrise, the girl hid from the sun in a cave, closing her ears against the sounds of mortal life. Six nights later they reached one of Everest's lower peaks and the Tibetan novice, jabbering in a mixture of Cantonese and Mandarin, showed them into a cemetery.

"This is spot chosen by Father General," he said.

The monk consulted a map. "Yes, it is."

"The holy brothers await us," said the Tibetan novice.

He led the girl and the monk along a twisting path flanked with gravestones. The sound of chanting filled the girl's ears, as loud and dreadful as the shrieking of a frightened baby at night. They were heading towards a chapel, a temple of Christian faith built in a Chinese style.

"You must watch the ceremony," said the monk to the girl. "It is your duty. I have made sure that there are no crucifixes in the place."

The girl smiled her acceptance. How could she tell him that crucifixes, like garlic, did not terrify her? She was not evil, despite her fangs and her marble white skin. She was merely different, like a traveller visiting a hostile place.

Four other novices were waiting in the chapel. They were dressed in saffron habits, another happy meeting of East and West. They had built a marble grave. It was open, the lid lying on the floor beside it. Their shovels were ranged neatly along a wall.

The monk took an urn out of his sack and held it up for the novices to see. Its silver sides glittered in the lamplight; the red seal glowed like a pool of fresh blood.

"Behold the remains of the Ancient One," said the monk.

The novices echoed his words in their own language. "I cast thee, evil spirit, into the tomb of oblivion," continued the monk. "May you never rise to torment God's true creations again."

He placed the urn in the shallow grave and the monks shovelled dirt on top of it, humming softly as they worked. The grave was sealed and a Star of David painted on its lid with silver paint. The monk turned his eyes towards the girl. "It is your turn now. Are you ready?"

She nodded, desperately trying to hold back the tears. The Tibetan novice led them out of the chapel to a humble crypt nearby. The monk opened a grate and they descended four steps into a small man-made cave. The stench of damp and rotting moss filled their nostrils.

The girl looked around her, her hand clamped over her nose. A tiny window at the back let in the pale moonlight. Through it she could see the branches of a magnolia in full bloom. The flowers glowed like pale moons, fragrant with pollen. They made her feel indescribably sad. Now that she was close to the moment, she found herself pining for the small things of mortal life; the scent of flowers, the taste of bread, the feel of warm woollen clothes against the skin.

The novices brought in a coffin made of cheap pine. They placed it in the middle of the floor, placing the lid against a wall. The girl could see her name carved in the wood: RUHA SLAVINKA, 1800 - 1813.

She climbed in and lay down. They had lined the coffin with lace from her mother's wedding gown, the gown she was meant to wear on her big day. I shall never marry now, she thought sadly. There is nothing left for me but loneliness and misery.

8

The monk placed an olive twig in her hands. "It was blessed by our Holy Father on Palm Sunday," he explained. "I have also sewn blessed olive leaves in the hem of your dress. As long as you keep the same garment, the Ancient One will not be able to harm you. But beware: remove the leaves and he will destroy you in an instant."

He stepped away from the coffin and pulled a crumpled sheet of paper from his pocket. One of the novices held a lamp close to his face, so he could read. "Do you, Ruha Slavinka, pledge to look after the Ancient One's ashes as long as they remain in their hiding place?"

"I do," replied the girl.

"And do you pledge to retrieve the said ashes should they be removed from their place of hiding?"

"I do."

"Then hear this. One of our fathers, a hypnotist practised in the art of suggestion has implanted a message in your brain. You will lie here asleep until someone touches the ashes. When and if that happens your mind will wake you up. It will direct you to the missing urn. May the good Lord have mercy on you and your lost soul."

The novices placed the lid on the coffin. The scent of freshly cut pine filled her nostrils. She concentrated on the smell, to stop herself from panicking.

"Try to sleep," said the monk, his voice

muffled by the wood. "It will make the time pass more quickly."

Goodbye, dear world, she thought sadly. I wanted so much and got so little. She wanted to weep, to release the enormous pain inside her but the tears refused to come. Vampires could not cry, she realised. They could only laugh. She closed her eyes and drifted off to sleep. The last thing she heard was the young novices nailing down the coffin lid.

iii

The five monks sat around a table in a monastery high above Ari Lasov, their faces hidden inside enormous cowls, prayer books clasped to their chests. Four of them were dressed in black robes; the fifth was all in white, denoting the rank of Father Superior.

"It is done," said one of the monks to the Superior. "I have buried the urn and the girl."

"And are you sure she will wake up if one of the urns is touched?" asked Father Superior.

"She will only leave her coffin if the urn in China is disturbed. But for the Ancient One to come back to life, all the four urns are needed. So we are safe."

Father Superior nodded in satisfaction. "Praise be to God. Many good people will sleep at peace in their beds tonight."

The monk pushed a scroll across the table. "Here is my map and your instructions. No one saw them except myself."

"And here are mine," said a second monk.

"And mine."

"And mine."

Father Superior picked up the scrolls with trembling, gnarled hands. Carefully, he unfurled them one by one and looked at them closely. There were no marks on them, no faint lines that betrayed the fact they had been traced or copied. Satisfied, he tucked them into a pigskin folder with a golden Star of David embossed on the front. "I shall burn them tonight," he said to the four monks. "I shall also destroy the book of instructions. No one will ever be able to trace the Ancient One's ashes. No one will ever be able to bring them back together again."

The other monks smiled, their fingers closed tightly around their prayer books. They stood to leave.

"Do not tell anyone about your mission," Father Superior warned them, "not even our brothers in the monastery. I have told the brethren you have been helping out with one of our seminaries in Rome. They will not question your absence."

"Our lips are sealed, Blessed Father." The Superior raised his old hands in benediction. "God bless you my sons. You have served our Holy Mother the Church and your Holy Order well. Praised be the Lord's name."

"Praised be the Lord's name." The monks left

the room, shutting the door behind them. Father Superior listened to their sandals creaking on the corridor floor. The sun was coming up behind the mountains. Light filtered into the study, illuminating the mahogany crucifix on the wall.

Father Superior opened the folder in front of him and took out a little red journal. He caressed it lovingly, for it was his favourite possession. His mother had given it to him on the day he had taken his holy vows. He had recorded all his thoughts in it, all his actions since joining the Holy Order. But now the book was tainted. He had filled its pages with notes and instructions for the disposing of the Ancient One's ashes. Father Superior looked at his handiwork. He had drawn up precise charts of the hiding places, based on knowledge he had acquired while travelling around the world on missionary work. He had painted detailed diagrams of the urns for the silversmith to copy: geometrical designs around the edges, with angels to be embossed in the red seals.

Father Superior sighed. The whole operation had been costly. It had sapped the Order of its money. He remembered the day the farmers from Ari Lasov had come knocking at his door, begging for help. How could he refuse them? His aim in life had always been to protect God's children from the evils of the world. So he had instructed them to burn the evil and seal his ashes in four silver urns. He had drawn elaborate plans for the urns' burials, involving many of the Order's houses around the world. Now the Order's bank account was overdrawn to the point of foreclosure. But the world was a safer place. And that was all that mattered to the Father Superior. The Order would have to earn some more money.

I shall burn the journal and the four maps in a salver, thought Father Superior, slipping it into the pigskin folder along with the maps and charts. We shall use the ashes for penance on Ash Wednesday. I shall cast...

A stab of pain shot through his chest, numbing his arm. His hand fluttered to his heart. The pain intensified, seeming to crush his chest. "Dear God, Saint Joseph and all the Saints..." He tried to rise but his feet had no strength. He fell forward, hitting his head on the table. "Dear Father, receive me into thine forgiving arms..." He had no time to finish his last prayer. A moment later the stroke paralysed his brain and he breathed his last.

The pigskin folder fell to the floor, the golden Star of David catching the morning light. Later that morning it was picked up by a novice, who gave it to Father Superior's surviving relatives along with the rest of his meagre possessions.

BURNING SECRET

Part 2

1996

Chapter 1

Tim Motton hurried along Erlington High Street, a new copy of Computer Weekly clamped firmly under one arm.

"Hello, Fatso," someone called from across the street. It was Simon Coote, a moronic boy from Tim's year at Erlington Comprehensive. "Have you snogged Nicola Cooper or Lin Yu Grant yet?"

Tim ignored his tormentor. He could have got into a squabble and called Simon Coote several names he deserved. But he wanted to get home as quickly as possible. There was some neat software on the CD-ROM given out free with Computer Weekly. He was desperate to try it out.

Tim got home and opened the front door with his own key. It was just gone four in the afternoon. Aunt Grace, who was looking after Tim while his mother was away, would not be home for an hour yet. Tim switched the kettle on and checked the post. Nothing from Mum. Or Dad. He sighed and spooned Bovril into a *Star Wars* mug. There were no biscuits in the tin, so he made himself a thick peanut butter sandwich with strawberry jam. When the kettle boiled, he put the food on a tray and carried it upstairs to his room.

There was E-mail waiting in his computer.

Tim flopped into his chair and accessed the first of two messages: Good afternoon, Mr Stoker. Seen any vampires lately?

Tim grinned and returned the message: Good afternoon, Deadhead. No, I haven't seen any vampires recently but my neck is feeling a bit sore. What do you think it could be?

PS: Have you found the Pincer Mania site on the World Wide Web yet? It's weird, just like most of the stuff on the 'net. It's all about deadly insects. Just deadly insects. I am sure the person who runs it is mentally unbalanced. But the graphics are brilliant. Check it out. The address is http://www.smg.pincer/prince/orbital.

Tim sent the message and accessed the second one. It was from a new subscriber to the Internet, looking for friends to talk to. Tim read his blurb:

Hi, I'm http/sun.txm/Haunted. I live in London and I am 13 years old. I attend Stoke Grammar School. I like reading Stephen King and Ramsey Campbell. I also like watching videos when my parents let me. On holiday, I snorkel and draw cartoons. I am looking to correspond with fans of horror fiction who also like computer animation and fantasy films. *Stargate* is my favourite film of all time.

There was a picture to go with the message. It showed a thin boy with huge, sorrowful eyes and ruffled blonde hair. He was standing in a graveyard, leaning against a green tombstone. Tim sent him a message:

Hello, Haunted. I'm Mr Stoker. I live in Erlington, a small village in Sussex, and I go to Erlington Comprehensive, which is fine if you ignore some of the brainless zombies that haunt its classrooms. I like reading Stephen King and Ramsey Campbell too but my favourite writer is M.R. James. He wrote some really spooky ghost stories back around the turn of the century which my dad used to read to me at bedtime. My dad is living with his new wife in Canada now. She's not a writer but she's got a very interesting job at the local morgue. My mum is a foreign correspondent with a national paper. She's out in the Middle East at the moment, covering some local skirmish or other. I'm staying with my Auntie Grace, who's Mark Dylan's house-keeper. Do you know Mark Dylan, the pop star? He comes from Erlington and he writes some really bloodthirsty lyrics for his songs. My best friends Nicola Cooper and Lin Yu Grant really like him. I prefer film soundtracks myself. What kind of music do you listen to? E-mail back and I'll give you the access codes to some weird and wonderful sites on the Internet.

Tim sent the message and turned to his sand-wich. Outside, a spring wind was teasing Aunt Grace's rhododendrons, ruffling their leaves.

It'll be dark soon, Tim thought. I wonder what time Auntie Grace will be home?

Chapter 2

The young farmer reached Shanghai shortly before nightfall. He had been walking all day and the sack on his right shoulder was getting heavier by the minute. He was thirsty too. It had been ten hours since he had bought his last cup of green tea from a small teahouse in the hills - and he had no money left for a fresh cup.

"Excuse me, miss," the farmer approached a young passer-by, forcing a shy smile on to his parched lips. "Can you tell me where Willow Street is?"

To his astonishment, the passer-by turned up her pert little nose, shook her head and moved on without saying a word.

City folk were dreadful, the farmer decided. They had no respect for the country people who grew their food and looked after their countryside.

"Excuse me, sir..." the farmer stopped an elderly gentleman in a stained velvet suit. "Can you tell me where Willow Street is?"

"No." The man glared and pushed the farmer out of his way.

The farmer sighed helplessly. He had to find Willow Street before nine or he would have to spend the night out on the streets with the vagrants. Someone was bound to steal his sack if he did. No one ever slept out on the streets without being robbed. Just then a policeman rode by on a bicycle, whistling a tune from one of the patriotic operas playing at the Shanghai Cultural Theatre. He took one look at the farmer's tattered clothes and stopped. "Can I help you?"

The young farmer's blood froze. He had no permission to be in the city. And he couldn't possibly tell the policeman where he was heading. "I am visiting my brother-in-law on Celebration Street," he lied.

The policeman held out a gloved hand. "May I see your identification papers, please?"

The farmer reached in his pocket and pulled out a crumpled yellow card. "Here you are, sir."

"What's your brother-in-law's name?" asked the policeman, giving the worn card a cursory glance.

"Liu Chian," stuttered the farmer, using the name of a friend back home in the mountains. "His sister, my wife, is sick. I thought I'd better tell him. I am sorry I haven't applied for permission to visit the city. It was an emergency."

The policeman handed the identity card back. "You don't need permission to visit the city," he said. "The law was changed a long time ago." He pointed to the sack on the farmer's shoulder. "What have you got in there? Mountain produce?"

"Turnips," said the farmer. "And a few carrots."

"No tobacco?"

"A little," said the farmer. He plunged his

arm in the sack and produced a small leather pouch. "Here, take it. I think my brother-in-law has given up smoking."

The policeman pretended to be shocked. "I couldn't possibly take bribes," he said.

"This is not a bribe," the farmer insisted. "It's a gift."

"Alright then." The policeman snatched the pouch and stuffed it inside his light blue jacket.

"Don't use it up all at once," grinned the farmer. "It will make your city throat sore." He slung his sack over his shoulder, smiling. "So long, then."

"So long." The policeman remounted his bicycle and sailed down the street, grinning. That was a close shave, the farmer thought. If the policeman had looked in his sack he would have put him under arrest. The farmer shuddered. How many years in work camp did a grave robber get? Ten? Twenty?

Someone poked him in the back, making him jump.

"A nice juicy rabbit for the missus, sir?"

The farmer turned to see an old livestock seller with a wicker cage strapped to her bent back. "Can you tell me the way to Willow Street?" he begged.

"That's in the posh part of town," said the old woman. "Keep on walking till you get to the Shanghai Prosperous Bank. Then turn left on to Petal Street and right again on to Mao Avenue. Willow Street is the second turning on the left."

"Thank you for your kindness." The young farmer bowed politely. "May seven years luck fill your cage."

The old woman cackled. "And may seven years prosperity fill your sack, you son-of-the-earth."

The young farmer hurried along the street. His thirst was almost unbearable now but the very thought of being so close to his destination kept him going. "In an hour's time, I'll be able to afford more than a cup of green tea," he said to himself. "I'll be rich enough to buy a bottle of expensive wine and a roast duck smothered in Hoisin sauce."

Ten minutes later he reached Willow Street. For a moment he stood on the pavement, watching hordes of well-dressed shoppers darting from one shop to another. Then he reached inside his left shoe and drew out a small card.

LIN PU
HERBAL REMEDIES
SPIRITUAL THERAPY
114 WILLOW STREET
SHANGHAI

The farmer started counting the numbers above the doors on the right side of Willow Street. Lin Pu's shop was right at the far end, tucked away between a fan shop and a big emporium selling kitchen utensils and wicker furniture. The farmer rang the bell.

"Yes?" An old man in a green silk robe answered the door, opening it just wide enough to peep out. "May I be of assistance?"

"I am looking for Mr Pu," said the farmer.

"I am he."

"I wish to purchase some essence of tranquillity," continued the farmer. "My wife is in need of sleep."

"Sleep comes only to the innocent," said Lin Pu. "Do you sleep well?"

"Like a cricket on a marble hearth," said the farmer.

Mr Pu opened the door wide. "Come in, Mr... "

"Ying," said the farmer. "My name is Huen Ying."

"I apologise for using such a long-winded password, Mr Ying," said Lin Pu. "Alas, it is necessary to keep out unwelcome spies."

"Don't worry, I understand," said Huen Ying. "My friend Lin Pao told me all about you. I have something you might be interested in buying."

"Wait a moment." Lin Pu locked the front door and drew bamboo shutters across the shop window. Then he switched off the lights. "Follow me, Mr Ying." He pushed aside a large cupboard, revealing a secret door. "Mind your head, now."

Huen Ying followed the old man down a staircase. "I hope you like what I've got for you," he said.

Lin Pu did not answer. He reached the

bottom of the staircase and switched on a dim light. "Welcome to my own secret heaven, Mr Ying," he chuckled.

The young farmer stared around him. Hundreds of golden Buddhas and slim porcelain ladies with painted cheeks stared back at him from rows upon rows of shelves.

"Do you like my collection?" asked Mr Pu.

Huen Ying was lost for words. Never had he seen so many riches amassed under one roof.

"I have enough treasures here to fill the Forbidden City itself," quipped Mr Pu. "Vases from the Ming Dynasty. Furniture used by Genghis Khan himself. You name it, Mr Ying, I have it."

"Who buys all these objects?"

"Foreign millionaires," said Mr Pu. "I help them ship it out of the country too." He led the way to the back of the vast shop and sat behind an ebony desk.

"Do you like it?" he asked the farmer.

Huen had never seen a desk before, so he didn't know what to say. "It was used by Marco Polo himself," boasted Mr Pu. "He wrote letters to the Roman Pope sitting in this chair."

Huen didn't know who Marco Polo or the Pope were either. "Would you like to see my treasure, Mr Pu?" he said.

He pulled a large parcel out of his sack. Mr Pu watched closely as he undid the binding and removed the muslin wrapping. "I'm not sure what it is," he said. "My wife found it while digging up potatoes last week." He placed the treasure on the desk. "There. It's a wonder she didn't smash it with the hoe."

Mr Pu stared at the object. It was a metal urn, its top covered with thick sealing wax. "May I?" He picked up the urn and blew on it gently. A swirl of dust rose from the lid, making him sneeze.

"It's solid silver," said Mr Pu. He rubbed one side of the urn with his sleeve. There were geometric patterns etched in the precious metal. Mr Pu guessed they had been designed by a European, probably in the early 19th century.

"Is it valuable?" Huen Ying asked.

"I have no idea yet." Mr Pu expertly dusted the sealing wax on the lid with a brush. It had been red once, but age had turned it a copper brown.

"More etchings," observed Huen. Mr Pu wiped the lid with a soft cloth. The etchings were clearly visible now. There were two angels carved in the wax. One held a mallet, the other a sharpened stake.

Mr Pu shuddered. "Where did you say your wife found this?"

"In the potato field."

"Come now, Mr Ying," chided Mr Pu. "Urns like this are not buried in farmer's graves. This came from a rich man's crypt. Did you steal it from a private cemetery, Mr Ying?"

Panic showed in the farmer's eyes. "I'm

telling you, my wife found it."

"Do not be afraid, Mr Ying," laughed Mr Pu, "I am not the police. In fact, you might say I am a criminal. The stuff you see around you was not donated to me by rich friends. It was sold to me by desperate people like you."

"Alright," said Huen. "I found the urn in a chapel."

"Found?"

"Stole. My wife is sick, you see. She hasn't been well since the second baby was born. We have no money for medicine. So I stole the urn from a chapel. A disused chapel. No one has been there for years. No one except my brother and I, that is. We discovered the chapel by accident when we were children. It was our secret playground. Still is."

Mr Pu unlocked the top drawer in his desk. "You are a very lucky man, Mr Ying," he said. "This urn is worth quite a bit."

"My ailing wife will be relieved."

Mr Pu counted out a large pile of paper money. "If you find anything else in that chapel, I would be interested in buying it."

"There is nothing else, I'm afraid," said Huen, putting the money carefully in his pocket. "My brother and I have looked all over the place."

"A pity." Mr Pu showed Huen back to the herbal shop on the ground floor. "Give my regards to your friend Pao," he said.

Huen waved goodbye and let himself out. Mr Pu locked the door behind him, then hurried back to the antique shop in the basement. The urn was still on his desk, its angels glowing a coppery brown in the lamplight.

"The guardians of creation help us," muttered Mr Pu to himself. He dipped the soft cloth in a jar of white spirit and continued to clean the lid. A few moments later he could see the shape of a coffin carved between the two angels. The lid was open, revealing a grinning corpse with evil, staring eyes. The point of the angels' sharpened stake was pointed directly at its heart.

Mr Pu got up and hurried to a display cabinet marked *Manuscripts*. His fingers trembled as he rifled through its contents, his eyes squinting to see in the gloom. He found an old pigskin folder and carried it back to the desk. Carefully, he opened it and pulled out some maps and a journal. He turned over the pages of the journal until he came to a picture of an urn, its lid sealed with sepia brown wax. "May the Lord Buddha have mercy on our souls!" cried Mr Pu. His heart beat wildly as he struggled to translate the Latin warning scribbled under the urn. He thought it said – HUMANS BEWARE THE GREATEST EVIL.

Chapter 3

Ruha opened her eyes with a snap. She had been asleep for nearly 200 years but instantly her mind was clear, her five senses sharply alert. Something outside her coffin had woken her up.

Slowly, Ruha turned her head and studied the dark around her. A bunch of woodlice were clinging to the coffin lid, only five inches away from her face. She blew on them gently and they scurried away in a blind panic.

Ruha pushed against the lid with her hands. There was a series of popping noises as the rusted nails broke in half. She sat up. A gust of cold wind hit her face. She breathed in deeply, relishing the taste of fresh air. It was good to be awake again. Nimbly, Ruha stepped out of the coffin. Even after nearly two centuries of lying prone in cramped conditions she did not feel the need to stretch or yawn. She merely stood there, her eyes scanning the dark like radars.

A million piercing noises assailed her ears. Insects crunched on the weeds around her. Moths fluttered through the humid air. In a corner, a terrified bumblebee shrieked as it desperately tried to free itself from the confines of a spider's web. Ruha approached the web. She could see the bee quite clearly in the dark. Its transparent wings made a miniature rainbow that shimmered and sparkled as they beat hopelessly against the sticky web. Gently, Ruha plucked the struggling insect free. Her action was followed by an angry hiss as the owner of the web realised it had been cheated of its dinner. Ruha ignored the spider. She set the bee down on the ground and watched it scuttle away to safety. Was this unlucky insect the reason why she had woken up from her two centuries of slumber, she wondered? Or had something else called her? Ruha struggled to remember. She had been asleep for so long...

An owl hooted in the dark outside. Ruha turned and saw a window. Beyond it was a gnarled magnolia, its flowers open in early bloom. Of course, she was lying in a crypt. In China. Memories came flooding back to her. She remembered the tall dark man standing on the road leading to Ari Lasov; the bite on her neck; the villager's hunt for the vampire; the burning of the evil one, the ashes in the urns. The urns. That's why she had woken up. Someone had touched one of the urns she was meant to be guarding.

Ruha hurried out of the crypt. The graveyard outside was covered in nettles and creeping ivy but her sharp eyes could still make out the inscriptions on the leaning tombstones:

Li Yu
beloved son of Martha Yu
died 1903
gone but never forgotten

Yen Ping
also Lao Ping
husband and wife

Ruha looked beyond the gravestones towards a chapel in the distance. Even in the dark, she could see that the door was wide open. A wild hare was sitting on the doorstep, tearing into a dandelion with sharp teeth. Ruha walked towards the chapel, her white hair glowing like snow. She could have flown if she had wanted to, but she preferred to use her feet. It made her feel more human.

The hare bolted as Ruha approached. Its fear saddened her. She had loved animals in her previous life. She had been especially fond of wild hares who sometimes came to nibble food from her hands.

Ruha entered the chapel. She could feel shards of marble under her bare feet. Someone had obviously vandalised the grave. Yes, there it was, right in the middle of the chapel, its marble lid smashed to bits with a mallet. Ruha picked her way through the sharp gravel and looked inside.

The urn had been stolen.

Ruha felt panic well in her chest. She had to get it back. She had promised the monks of Ari Lasov that she would guard the four urns forever...

Outside the chapel Ruha raised her slender arms to the waning moon. A strong breeze ruffled her white hair, tugged at her robe. "Let me get it back," she begged. "Oh God, let me get the urn back."

A sudden stab of pain shot through her thin body, making her gasp. Her feet flew from the ground and her arms grew long and strangely numb. She tried to cry out but only a strange squeak escaped her mouth. The wind lifted her up, like a vine leaf in autumn. She looked down at her shadow: she had changed into a bat.

Chapter 4

Miss Harman looked round the class expectantly. "Has anyone chosen a topic for their summer project yet?" she asked. "It's the last day of the term, you know." Tim Motton put his hand up right away.

"Blabbermouth," hissed Simon Coote.

"That's enough of that, Simon," said Mrs Harman. "Tell us about your idea, Timothy."

"Nicola Cooper, Lin Yu Grant and I have decided to do a project on Mark Dylan, the pop star," said Tim. The rest of the class groaned.

"Mark Dylan is so sad," said Frieda, a tall redhead with a white hairband.

"His lyrics are dreadful," added Simon.

"They're not," said Lin Yu.

Miss Harman groaned. Inwardly she agreed with Simon. Mark Dylan's lyrics were dreadful. All blood and guts and morose self-pity. But, Miss Harman decided, Tim always came up with a new angle on clichéd subjects. "What drew you to this particular topic, Lin?" she asked.

"Mark Dylan is the only famous person to come out of Erlington," said Lin. "We are going to find out what made him want to become a pop star and what makes him stay in the village despite his worldwide success."

"That's a very interesting approach," said Miss Harman. "Most pop stars move to London once they have made it big. How do you plan to gather your material?"

"Tim's aunt is Mark's housekeeper," Nicola cut in. "She's going to let us take pictures of his house. We've also got some interviews taken from newspapers and magazines."

"That's great," said Miss Harman. "You can learn a lot about a person from his house. Perhaps you should interview Tim's aunt too. She might know a lot more about Mark than the newspaper people who write about him. I believe Mark Dylan is a recluse. He only gives interviews when he releases a new song or an album. Now has anybody else settled on a subject?"

Before anyone could answer, the bell rang. Everyone in Class E shoved their english textbooks into their bags and headed for the door.

"Those of you who have not settled on a topic yet can choose one from the list I gave you yesterday," said Miss Harman chirpily. "Enjoy your summer holidays, everyone." Only Lin Yu answered. "You too, Mrs Harman."

Ruha stood in the shadow of a doorway in Hong Kong and watched people hurrying past her. No one seemed to notice her; perhaps they couldn't see her.

Ruha had learnt a lot about herself in the last

few nights. She had discovered that she could change her shape at will, just by thinking. She had already spent many hours flying as a bat. She had travelled all the way from a cemetery on Mount Everest, 5000 feet above sea level, to the city of Kowloon in Hong Kong. It had been difficult at first. Her thoughts kept drifting back to her human form, causing her to fall out of the sky. But eventually she had mastered the art of transformation. She had even discovered she could change into an insect. Perhaps being a vampire was not so bad after all.

A woman and child passed by, the child crying for sweets. The woman stopped to pull a bag out of her pocket. The child laughed and hugged his mother's waist. The mum, smiling, ruffled his thick hair.

Instantly Ruha changed her mind about being a vampire. It suddenly dawned on her that she would never be hugged or kissed again. All the people she knew were long dead. All except one. The Ancient One. He was only sleeping, and now there was a danger that he might come back. Ruha could smell his impending presence in the air. Perhaps all vampires were bonded together with this feeling. What was it? Fear? Survival?

Ruha closed her eyes and focused her thoughts on the missing urn. In her mind's eye she could see it very clearly: it was lying on a mahogany desk next to some books. Ruha forced her thoughts to show her the titles. They

were english. The urn was in England, then.
That's where Ruha had to go.

Chapter 5

Mrs Arnold was making a call on her mobile phone when the jeep came over the icy knoll. "They're here, Gerald," she barked into the mouthpiece. "I've got to go." She switched off the phone and thrust it into the pocket of her fur-lined jacket. "Malcolm, you're late," she called as she strode towards the jeep. "I called Gerald to see what was going on. This is just not good enough."

"I'm sorry," said Malcolm, a young man with long blonde hair tied into a ponytail. "We had to wait for the explosives to be delivered. We set off as soon as we could. None of my crew have had any breakfast or lunch."

"There's no time for a lunch break now," snapped Mrs Arnold. "We have to get to destination A before dark." Without waiting for an answer, she turned and started walking back towards her own vehicle, a large state of the art truck with the word CATERPILLAR stencilled across the hood. Mr Ping, Vietnamese archaeologist, whom Mrs Arnold referred to condescendingly as "the guide", opened the door for her.

Malcolm turned to his colleagues. "I'm sorry about this," he said under his breath. "We'll have to grab a health bar and a cup of coffee as we go along." His colleagues, six men in fur-lined parkas and snow goggles, nodded. None of them complained. Mrs Arnold was testing their patience to the limits. She was even breaking union rules and safety procedures in her relentless race against time. But she was paying the men a fortune for it. Plus bonuses if they got whatever Mrs Arnold wanted within a specific period of time.

As the green jeep followed Mrs Arnold's vehicle, the men wondered what it was they had come to the Arctic to look for. Malcolm, their immediate employer, had merely told them that Mrs Arnold was in search of three different things hidden in three different parts of the world. What they were he did not say. And the men had not dared ask. But now they were getting curious. The whole enterprise was shrouded in secrecy. Mrs Arnold had made them all sign papers preventing them from talking to their friends or newspaper reporters. Not even their wives and families knew where they were.

Malcolm poured hot coffee from a thermos flask and passed around some oat and nut bars. The men ate and sipped in silence, each of them watching the snowy landscape outside. The jeep made hardly any noise as its special tyres ploughed through the ice.

"How long is it before we get to destination A?" one of the men asked Malcolm. The boss checked his watch. "Ten minutes," he said. "Fifteen, if the ice gets harder as the sun sets."

"It'll be dark in two hours' time," said one of

the men. "What exactly do we have to do when we get there?"

"I have no idea," Malcolm said. "Mrs Arnold is keeping the deck close to her chest."

"Typical," said one of the men, an explosives expert with red hair and prescription glasses. He wiped the steam off the jeep window and looked at the landscape outside again. "Not exactly a theme park, is it?" he complained.

"Not unless you're a penguin," laughed one of his colleagues, a mountain climber who had once worked for a famous circus. He squirmed in his seat. "I need to go to the loo, boss."

"I'm afraid we can't stop now," said Malcolm. "Mrs Arnold is already spoiling for a fight as it is."

"What's up with her, anyway?" muttered the explosives expert. "She's been on edge ever since we left England."

"More to the point, who is she, and who employs her?" added his colleague.

Malcolm ignored the men's probing questions. He knew who Mrs Arnold was and who employed her but he had no idea what she was looking for. Or who was paying for this expensive expedition. He suspected it was a Middle Eastern government. Or perhaps it was a South American dictator attempting to find a uranium mine. Malcolm hadn't given the matter much thought. All he cared about was the fact that he was being paid half a million pounds sterling to mastermind the operation. With a fee like that, Malcolm couldn't care less if Mrs

Arnold's sponsor was looking for the Holy Grail itself.

The Caterpillar truck pulled to a halt. Malcolm's men tumbled out of the jeep, stretching their stiff limbs. They were standing at the bottom of a huge, frozen cliff. There were no trees around them, just miles and miles of frozen plain. The setting sun reflecting off the ice was blinding. Even with special goggles on, the mens' eyes ached.

Mrs Arnold marched over to Malcolm, a map fluttering from her gloved hand. "We're going in there," she said. "Please have the men follow us with their equipment." Malcolm looked puzzled, for Mrs Arnold was pointing to the cliff face.

"There is a doorway," explained Mr Ping. "We must find it."

He pulled a sonar detector out of his pocket and moved along the cliff face, his eyes fixed firmly on the ice. "Should be here," he said.

Mrs Arnold followed him, her snowboots leaving deep footprints in the snow behind her. Malcolm instructed his men to bring explosives, some digging tools and climbing gear. He himself carried a box of emergency supplies, flares and a first-aid kit. They all followed the guide, looking for signs of a doorway under the ice.

"Here it should be," cried Mr Ping at last. Mrs Arnold halted. "Malcolm," she commanded.

Malcolm studied the spot Mr Ping was

pointing to. There was no sign of anything under the thick crust of ice.

"Is there," Mr Ping assured him. "Trust me."

"Alright." Malcolm barked instructions at his men. They snapped to attention quickly and silently, like soldiers doing manoeuvres. Within minutes, small niches had been carved in the ice and explosives placed in them. Fuses were laid. The explosives expert stabbed buttons on a hand-held micro detonator. "We've got exactly five minutes," he said.

The men, followed by Mr Ping and Mrs Arnold, retreated to the safety of their vehicles. Precisely a minute later the charges erupted. The cliff face seemed to shake and massive sheets of solid ice hurtled to the ground, smashing on impact like enormous glass panes. A white mist rose out of the centre of the explosion, covering the windscreen of both vehicles in a thin sheet of snowflakes.

"Is there!" cried Mr Ping. He leapt out of the truck and ran to the cliff face. Mrs Arnold and the men followed. A gaping doorway had indeed appeared in the ice.

"Report time," barked Mrs Arnold. She turned on a small Dictaphone and spoke into it rapidly. "Reached destination A at 18.00 hours local time. Approach through tunnel, entrance facing 55 degrees west. Expecting to find Object Alpha within one hour."

An hour? Malcolm frowned and looked at his wristwatch.

"Stephanie," he began. "The men have been on duty for 18 hours..."

"We'll be done soon," snapped Mrs Arnold. She turned to the men herself, giving them a fake smile. "Follow me, lads."

The men lit torches and hurried into the tunnel. The air inside it was damp and clammy compared to the dry iciness on the plain. Mr Ping coughed, beating his puny chest with his fist.

"Tunnel goes deep, deep into the cliff," he informed the rest of the group. Hearing this, Malcolm stopped to spray a large circle of day-glo paint on a wall. If the tunnel suddenly turned into a confusing maze, he knew the glowing signs would help the party find its way out again.

"Hurry up," Mrs Arnold urged him. Malcolm glared and obeyed. Mr Ping was almost running now. The men could see his torch bobbing up and down in the dark like a drunken firefly.

"We are there," he shouted triumphantly.

Mrs Arnold turned to Malcolm. "Have your team wait here, please. No one is to come any further." She waited until all the men had stopped walking and Malcolm was passing round cups of hot coffee. Then she followed Mr Ping out of the tunnel.

The Vietnamese archaeologist was standing in a round temple, his bald head bathed in the light of his own torch. "Isn't it beautiful?" he cried.

Mrs Arnold didn't reply. 'Beautiful' was not quite the right term that sprang to her mind.

'Spooky' was more appropriate.

"You could fit two St. Paul's cathedrals in here," said Mr Ping. He shone his torch on a row of statues decorating the round wall. "Look at those faces. None of them are recognisable. These gods have not been worshipped in any country or civilisation we know."

"Where is the crypt?" Mrs Arnold wanted to know.

"My guess is there's a flight of steps behind the main altar," said Mr Ping. "But I might be wrong. I have never seen a temple like this in all my years of archaeological research."

Mrs Arnold ignored his excited babble and marched towards the main altar. She found the steps to the crypt right behind it, nestled between two statues of praying women. "Wait for me there, Mr Ping," she ordered. Clutching her torch, she climbed down the slippery steps, her hiking boots making no noise as they sank in wet moss.

The crypt was small and claustrophobic, like an airless cell in a high-security jail. There was only one grave in it. Mrs Arnold placed her torch on a ledge and looked around her. The walls were covered in bas-relief carvings of bats and wolves. A mosaic of a girl with white hair was set in the low ceiling. She looked sad, her hands held up in prayer towards the skies. Mrs Arnold touched the girl's face for a moment then turned her attention to the grave. It looked just like the picture in her sponsor's book: a raised sarcophagus decorated with golden images of more bats. There was an inscription carved on the top but Mrs Arnold had no time or desire to read it. She pulled a crowbar out of her backpack and forced the grave open. As she had expected, there was no corpse or skeleton inside: just an old urn covered in moss and lichen.

Mrs Arnold picked up the urn and wiped the moss off the lid. The red seal was intact. It showed two angels kneeling over an open grave. One held a mallet, the other a sharpened stake. They were both looking down at an evil figure lying in the grave.

Mrs Arnold put the urn in her backpack. Then she switched on her Dictaphone. "Object Alpha found at exactly 19.00 hours," she said triumphantly. "Mission 1 accomplished."

Ruha lay in a crate at the back of a deserted warehouse, waiting for the sun to set. She missed her coffin, especially the security it gave her. Outside, mortals moved about their daily business, shouting to each other in a strange tongue Ruha could not understand.

The second urn had been moved. Ruha was sure of it. When she closed her eyes, she could see it, white and gleaming as if somebody had just polished it. No doubt it would soon join the first urn on the mahogany desk in England.

That meant someone was trying to bring the four urns together.

The terrible Ancient One was coming back.

Ruha shivered. How long would it take her to get to England? And when she got there, how could she get the urns back? Perhaps she needed to enlist the help of a mortal, someone who understood the ways of the modern world, someone who could use these new inventions to stop the Ancient One.

Ruha opened the crate and stepped out. The sun had set completely and the warehouse was in darkness. She tiptoed to a window. The street outside was faintly illuminated with electric light. Harmless light. Ruha stepped out and shut the warehouse door behind her.

A few minutes later she was in Wan Chai district, the very heart of Hong Kong's commercial district. The light here was dazzling, spilling out of large emporiums that lined both sides of every street. Neon signs flashed on and off continuously.

Ruha looked in a shop window. The shop sold large boxes with flickering, coloured pictures. Sometimes the pictures changed into writing. Ruha concentrated her thoughts. Something in her mind told her that the boxes were miracle machines used for various jobs. Mortals could write and store documents in them. They could use them for drawing pictures and doing elaborate calculations. Best of all they could use them for sending messages halfway across the world.

Ruha opened her eyes and smiled. She could use the machines to contact a suitable mortal, someone in England who lived close to the urns. Then, somehow, she had to get there herself.

She lifted her arms, willing herself to change into a bat. Her mind directed her to Kai Tak airport.

Chapter 6

Before meeting Lin Yu, Auntie Grace had lived under the mistaken impression that all Chinese people were shy and retiring. Lin Yu had changed all that. She was loud, bossy and, in Auntie Grace's opinion, domineering.

"You've got to let us into Mark's house," she insisted. "We promised Miss Harman we would do our summer project about him."

Auntie Grace turned to Tim. "But do you have to get inside the house? Can't you just copy something out of a magazine? *Hello* is always doing stories on Mark's mansion."

"We need a new angle, Mrs Motton," said Nicola politely. "We want to find out why Mark stayed in Erlington."

"He doesn't stay in Erlington all the time," argued Aunt Grace. "He's got a penthouse flat in London too. That's where he conducts most of his business."

"But his real home is here," said Lin Yu. "His famous artefact collection is in Erlington."

Auntie Grace got up to put the kettle on. "I don't know. It's more than my job is worth."

"Please, Mrs Motton," said Nicola. "We'll promise to be careful. We won't touch anything, honest."

Auntie Grace frowned. Nicola Cotten was a nice, sensible girl. She lived with her mum out on the Grasslands Estate, looking after her younger brothers and sisters when her mum was on late shift at the hospital. With Nicola in the group, perhaps she could trust Tim and Lin Yu to visit Mark's house.

"Alright," she said. "You can come next week while he's recording his new song in the States. But I don't want you poking around in his bedroom. And I don't want you touching anything on the desk in his study either. Apparently some of the knick-knacks there are worth thousands."

Tim lay in bed, staring up at the ceiling. Something had woken him up. He turned on his side and looked at the alarm clock on his bedside cabinet. It was two thirty-five in the morning. Tim groaned. What had disturbed him?

A flashing green light caught his attention. It was the computer. Someone was trying to contact him.

Tim trudged out of bed and accessed the message: HUMANS BEWARE THE ULTIMATE EVIL. The words quivered, as if the power supply to the computer was getting weak.

"There's a weirdo on the loose," Tim groaned. "And he's got hold of my E-mail address." He pulled the computer plug out of the socket and returned to bed.

Five minutes later he was snoring loud enough to wake the dead.

Chapter 7

A magnificent black bird appeared in the sky, its rotating wings reflecting the sunlight like water in a fall.

"Eh-la," shouted Riccardo. "The white people are coming."

"Stay here, don't move," commanded Mr Ping. He hurried towards a launch pad, his right hand clamped firmly over his hat. The helicopter landed as he came out of the trees, the roar of its engine scaring the life out of a multitude of birds. "Good morning, Mrs Arnold."

"Good morning." Mrs Arnold smiled weakly. She had lost weight since the last time Mr Ping had seen her. Her hair was slightly longer; it had lost some of its lustre. "Bad day?" asked Mr Ping.

"No," said Mrs Arnold, "I just haven't slept for three days, that's all."

"Ah," said Mr Ping. "Perhaps Mrs Arnold should rest before the next journey."

Mrs Arnold scowled. "No, Mr Ping, I want to get to destination B as soon as is humanly possible. Are Malcolm and the boys here?"

"The boys are all ready," confirmed Mr Ping. "We must go." He blew a whistle and Riccardo came running. "Please leave right away."

"Sí, señor." Riccardo turned and disappeared back in the bush. Mr Ping turned to Mrs Arnold. "Riccardo is the best guide in all Peru. He knows this jungle like the back of his hand."

Mrs Arnold smiled icily again. "Then perhaps Riccardo can get us to the temple before the end of the week."

"The journey takes only one day on foot," confirmed Mr Ping. "The path is too small for car or horses."

"Very well."

Riccardo came back with four other Peruvians in tow. Malcolm appeared with his men, all six of them dressed in khaki shorts and safari hats. "Hello, Mrs Arnold," he said. "We're all set to go." The others nodded, unsure if they should speak.

"Good," said Mrs Arnold. "We're leaving at once." The group left the encampment without a word, like a class of school children going in the school hall for assembly. Riccardo led the way with two of his men, both armed with antiquated rifles and extra ammunition. Malcolm's men carried the usual equipment: ingredients for explosives; climbing ropes and first-aid kits. Mrs Arnold only had her back-pack, in which she kept her mobile phone, her Dictaphone and a clean pair of socks. Riccardo's other two men brought up the rear with the food packs, keeping a lookout for wild animals.

For five hours they followed the contours of a slow-moving river, often stopping to drink from their water bottles. Shortly after noon, they halted for lunch: a vegetable stew heated over a naked fire by one of Riccardo's men. Their hunger satisfied, they resumed their course, leaving the banks of the river and striking out into the dense bush. Soon they couldn't see the sky anymore. There was a permanent smell of damp undergrowth in the air; invisible birds called to each other, large moths fluttered in the greenery.

"Es el espíritu de la jungla," said Riccardo.

"What does he mean?" asked one of Malcolm's men.

"He said it is the spirit of the jungle," Mr Ping interpreted.

The man looked blank. "What is?"

"The noise. He thinks it is caused by the spirit of the jungle."

"No slacking, gentlemen," cut in Mrs Arnold. "We are running three hours late already." She walked briskly alongside Malcolm who marched on solemnly without saying a word.

Towards evening the forest thinned out and the sky reappeared. The group stopped for the night and Malcolm inflated hi-tech sleeping tents with built-in heating systems. Riccardo's men heated up more vegetable stew, stirring in ground pinto beans and maize to make it go further. Mrs Arnold ate an apple and drank a protein meal made with milk and powder. Mr Ping, who was fasting, refused all food. He sat apart from the rest, poring over maps and notes in his organiser.

Early the next morning they bathed in a pool, had a breakfast of health bars and coffee and set off again. Riccardo's guides chatted amongst themselves, pointing out poisonous frogs which they instantly trampled to death with their boots. By late morning they were all weary and exhausted.

"Not far now," said Mr Ping encouragingly. "We are close to destination B."

He was right. Shortly afterwards the thinning forest gave way to cleared land. It was all overrun with weeds and young trees but you could still make out that it had once been cultivated.

"Esta tierra es buena," explained Riccardo.

"He means this land is good for corn," interpreted Mr Ping. "Not worked for a long time now. Something scares the locals away."

Mrs Arnold shot him an icy glare. "Mr Ping," she said, "please leave the superstitions to the natives. We are running late."

Suitably chastised, Mr Ping led the way through the overgrown fields. Riccardo's men followed at a wary distance, gabbling to each other and gesticulating wildly.

"What's the matter?" asked Mrs Arnold.

"The men refuse to come any further," explained Riccardo. "They say the place you are going to is full of evil spirits."

"Nonsense," snapped Mrs Arnold. "It's just a ruined temple."

Riccardo looked helpless. "They say the place is haunted by...by...walking dead."

Mrs Arnold turned to Mr Ping angrily. "You engaged them," she said. "You sort this out."

Mr Ping spoke to Riccardo in Spanish. The

guide nodded and shook his head. His men crowded round, listening intently. "Alright," said Riccardo at last. "We'll go. But we must be paid the extra in cash."

Mr Ping beamed and patted him on the shoulder. "Good man. You deserve rewarding." The group resumed its journey. It was now quite obvious to Malcolm's men that destination B was a ruined Inca temple. They could already see its roof jutting out above the trees. The heat was intolerable, making Mr Ping sweat profusely. Malcolm's men located a storeroom and stopped to rest in its cool interior.

"Your men are to wait here in case I need them," said Mrs Arnold to Malcolm after they'd all had cold coffee. "I have no idea what lies ahead."

Mr Ping smiled, wiping his brow with an enormous scarf. "We might need to blow up the grave. Perhaps the wall too." He consulted a diagram in his organiser. "This way, please Mrs Arnold."

Mrs Arnold followed him out into the blinding sunshine. The pair crossed an enormous courtyard and entered a massive building with sloping, tiered walls. Mr Ping stopped to inspect a statue with a solemn face. "It's beautifully carved," he observed. "Best quality craftsmanship." Mrs Arnold said nothing. She pulled a torch out of her bag and shone it on the wall.

"We go down this corridor," said Mr Ping. He put his organiser away and started walking. Mrs

Arnold wiped her face with a handkerchief. "There's a door ahead," cried Mr Ping. "I came only this far last week with guides. From now on it's all new."

Mrs Arnold switched on her Dictaphone. "The time is now 15.45," she said. "Approaching destination B."

Mr Ping turned right into a low room. "Look," he whispered reverently. "Inca symbols. Maize. Corn. Bananas…"

He pointed to a small niche right in the middle of a north facing wall. "…bat. Not an Inca symbol."

"We seem to be on the right track, then," said Mrs Arnold, unable to hide her excitement. She thrust the torch under her left arm and touched the bat. The head seemed to be loose.

"It's a key," cried Mr Ping.

Mrs Arnold pressed the bat's head and a section of the wall swung open, revealing a dark, musty tunnel. "No need for Malcolm's explosives," said Mr Ping. He hurried down the tunnel, his torch lighting up the way. Mrs Arnold followed, swiping at thick spiders webs with her bare hands.

"We're here," Mr Ping said. He stepped out into a small underground graveyard, his voice sounding faint and hollow. "At least five thousand people are packed in here. Look." He pointed to a cluster of large holes carved in the round wall. "Dead people like sardines. Whole families. Little babies too."

"How are we going to find Object Beta?"

demanded Mrs Arnold. Mr Ping shrugged. "Look for a bat carving."

"Very well." Mrs Arnold started to inspect the gaping holes. Skulls with hollow eyes stared vacantly back at her. Teeth gleamed in the torchlight like pearls. "The dead are not Inca," Mr Ping informed her from across the graveyard. "People buried here have other religions. Mysterious..."

Mrs Arnold was in no mood to discuss world religions. She was getting worried in case Malcolm decided to come and look for her. "Step on it, Mr Ping."

The archaeologist waggled his torchlight. "It's here. It's here." Mrs Arnold hurried over, nearly tripping over a skeleton lying on the floor. Mr Ping was shining his torch on a stone bat carved above one of the holes. She put her backpack on the ground. "Wait outside please, Mr Ping."

Mr Ping left her, a sullen expression on his childlike face. She waited until he was outside the graveyard, then poked her right hand in the hole. Her fingers met a ribcage draped in thick spiders webs. A fat beetle scuttled out of a child's skull and ran across her hand, its wings trembling. Mrs Arnold did not flinch. She kept on feeling in the dark until her fingers located the urn. Then she switched on her Dictaphone and spoke into it with a satisfied grin: "Object Beta found at 17.02, 12th July 1995."

Chapter 8

"Now don't you dare touch anything," warned Auntie Grace.

Tim sighed patiently. "Don't worry, Auntie Grace. We won't touch a thing."

"We promised we wouldn't," added Lin Yu cheekily.

Auntie Grace poured herself a cup of tea and sat down at the kitchen table. "Mark is fussy about his things," she mumbled, opening her evening paper.

Ignoring her, Tim, Nicola and Lin Yu left the kitchen. Nicola was very excited about being in Mark Dylan's house. She was a big fan of the singer even though she had never admitted it to her friends at school. Lin Yu wasn't as keen. She preferred classical music to pop or rock. Her mother had always listened to Bach or Vivaldi while relaxing, and Lin Yu had grown up with the same tastes.

"This is the dining room," said Tim, turning on the lights. Nicola's eyes nearly popped out of her head. "You could seat an army round that table."

"Thirty, to be exact," said Tim. "Auntie Grace says the cutlery is all black."

Lin Yu made a face. "Not in the best of taste, is it?"

"Rock stars are expected to be over the top," said Tim. "Believe me, this is restrained compared to excesses of other millionaires."

Nicola took some pictures of the dining table and several limited edition prints on the wall. "Let's see the study next," said Lin Yu.

"Alright." Tim turned off the lights and showed the girls down a long corridor.

"Chilly," said Nicola.

"Probably haunted too," quipped Lin Yu.

"Most Gothic manors are haunted, actually," said Tim. "This one is meant to have a headless nun in the library."

Nicola's eyes lit up. "Where's that?"

"Upstairs," said Tim. "Let's see the study first." He opened a big oak door. "It's big enough to be a public library, isn't it?"

"Or a concert hall," Nicola said.

"The flagstones are original," Tim explained. "So is the huge fireplace. Aunt Grace says the first owners used to roast a whole pig in it. Of course, it wasn't a study then. It was a family room where rich people ate informal suppers, relaxed, and played card games and pool."

"Look at all these things," said Lin Yu. "It's like an antique shop in here." They moved around Mark's famous collections of strange artefacts from around the world, inspecting things they never even knew existed.

"There's a coffin here," said Nicola.

"You're kidding," said Lin Yu. "That's sick, seriously sick."

"Not as sick as this," laughed Tim. He was pointing to a dead monkey floating in a jar of formaldehyde. The poor monkey was all hunched up, as if it had actually died in the jar.

"What's he want that for?" wondered Nicola, snapping away.

"Inspiration, he'd say," said Lin Yu. "And what are these?"

"Victorian curiosities," replied Tim. "They used to glue the bleached bones of different animals together to make up mythical animals. The Victorians were obsessed with death."

Nicola took more pictures, moving around to get different angles.

"Where's Mark's desk?" asked Lin Yu.

"Over there." The three of them hurried across the vast room. "Look, sheet music," said Nicola, excited. Mark must be working on a new song.

"Look at this letter opener," exclaimed Lin Yu. "It's got a boar's head. And what's this?"

"A silver compass," said Tim. "To draw circles with."

Lin Yu pointed to three silver urns, standing in a neat row next to a pigskin folder. "What could these be?"

"Burial urns," said Tim. "They look ancient. Worth a fortune, no doubt."

"You mean there's human ashes inside?" Lin Yu giggled to hide her unease. "How awful. This guy needs therapy."

"All artists are a bit strange," said Tim. "That's what makes them creative." He turned to Nicola. "Take a picture."

Nicola moved close to the urns and pressed

the shoot button. The flash bounced off the polished silver like a bolt of lightning, making them jump out of their skin.

"You alright?" asked Tim, startled.

"Yeah." Nicola rubbed her eyes.

Just then they heard a terrible howl. It sounded like a wounded dog baying at the moon. "What's that?" said Nicola, her blood running cold.

The animal howled again, twice. It sounded like it was in the house. The kids shivered.

"I wonder what's in the pigskin folder?"

The man in the black suit smiled at Ruha. "May I have your landing card, please?"

Ruha looked puzzled. The man smiled and thrust a white card at her. "Fill this in."

Ruha shrugged, trying to understand what he wanted. The man sighed patiently. "Can you speak English? No?" He beckoned with his hands, like a man coaxing a puppy out from under an armchair. "Come this way, please."

Ruha followed him to a small cubicle with a narrow window. What did he want? Why did he not let her just go to the people who were going to help her? She had had no trouble getting out of Hong Kong. She had merely changed herself into a fly and smuggled herself aboard a plane bound for Gatwick Airport. Regrettably, the effort of staying a fly had been too much for her.

Her concentration had wavered after a few hours. She changed back into a girl and slipped into an empty seat. Luckily the flight was only half full. No one had noticed her...

"What language do you speak?" The man in the black suit was talking to her again. He was an official of some kind.

"What lan-guage?"

"Yes, what country do you come from?"

She couldn't understand a word he was saying. Foreign words seemed to tumble out of his mouth like a waterfall, all joined together with no pauses in between. She tried communicating directly with his subconscious mind, which knew all languages, but he was too busy gabbling to understand her.

"Wait a minute," he said. "I'll get an interpreter." He hurried out of the room, his shoes squeaking on the polished floor.

Ruha settled back in her chair. She had to get out of here. The third urn had been brought to England. Only one more to go and the world was in danger. She had to escape.

Ruha stood up and imagined herself an insignificant little death's-head moth.

Lin Yu sat on Tim's bed, tapping on a notebook with the end of her pencil. Lin Yu never used pens to make notes. Journalists in films always used pencils. It made the notes less permanent and left them open to change. Open to discussion. "What are we going to tackle first?" she asked.

"Perhaps we could describe Mark Dylan's childhood here in Erlington," said Tim, staring at his computer.

"Great," said Nicola, who was sitting in an old armchair by the window. "There's something about that in last week's issue of *Smash Hits*. Mark's got a new album coming out soon. It's called *Say Hello To Eternity*." She flicked though the magazine. "Here it is: Mark Dylan was born in Erlington in 1958. His father was an undertaker..."

"I bet he made that up," said Lin Yu, "to fit in with his macabre image."

"Possibly," Tim agreed. "Perhaps we should investigate that. Talk to a few locals about Mark's age. His father moved away to live with his sister in Newcastle a couple of years ago, I think."

"Right." Nicola wrote a reminder in her notebook with her bendy pen. Unlike Lin Yu, Nicola wrote all her notes in ink, so they wouldn't accidentally get rubbed out. Nicola hated doing anything twice, especially writing notes. She picked up *Smash Hits* again and read some more. "Mark's mother used to tell him the most gruesome bedtime stories."

"That's sick," interrupted Lin Yu.

"It's not," said Tim. "My father used to tell me ghost stories at bedtime."

He was interrupted by a bleep from the

computer. All three turned to the glowing blue screen. A vibrating red dot, the shape of a drop of blood, had appeared in the middle of it.

"Oh no," said Tim. "A virus."

The dot grew bigger, erasing the words Tim had just typed. The entire screen turned a bright, pulsating red. Tim tried pulling the modem plug out of the telephone socket but it made no difference. The red just got brighter and brighter until it was almost blinding. Then four letters in large, black, Gothic script appeared on the screen.

They spelt the word HELP.

Chapter 9

The dry water well lay roughly in the middle of the Sahara desert, in a small oasis that had for years welcomed thirsty Bedouins and nomads. Mr Ping had travelled there with a group of camel herders from Benghazi, pretending to be a photographer on assignment for the *Middle East Economic Digest*. The desert people had shown him straight to the well, without the use of the map he had been given by Mrs Arnold. The oasis was a famous one, they had told him. It had saved many a life in the past. The Bedouins called it Gebel El Risq - the Stones of Luck.

"There is your well," they said, pointing to a hole no larger than a manhole. "It is dry now. The curse of the infidel is upon it."

Mr Ping looked down the dark shaft. It seemed to be bottomless. This is a job for Malcolm and the boys, he decided, heading towards the shelter of a tent.

Malcolm and his crack team of experts arrived two days later, in a battered army jeep. They measured the well with a sonar device, erected a steel and polycarbonate motorised winch above it and lowered a cable-fibre rope. Mrs Arnold arrived in a helicopter just as they were securing the rope to a lightweight aluminium cage. She was dressed in a white cotton dress, with long sleeves to protect her arms from the fierce desert sun. Her nose and cheeks were covered in blue reflective make-up. It made her look like an ageing surfer in California. Malcolm's men grunted "good morning" begrudgingly as she approached. Mr Ping bowed politely.

"Ready to go?" she asked.

Mr Ping nodded. "The next Arab caravan is due tonight," he informed the group. "We must leave before. Bedouins are very superstitious. We must not wake the spirit of the well. He will make trouble for the Bedouins. Kill all their camels and goats."

"We'd better get a move on, then," said Malcolm. "We mustn't upset the Bedouins. They could make life very difficult for us. Do you want my men to escort you to the bottom of the well, Mrs Arnold?"

She shook her head. "Let Ping and I have a look first. We'll call you if we need you." She opened the cage door and stepped inside, clutching her backpack. Malcolm handed her a bright yellow helmet with a flashlight attached.

"An English miner's helmet," said Mr Ping.

"Not quite," laughed Malcolm, "although the general principle is the same. You'll find that the flashlight will turn itself on automatically, the moment it becomes too dark to see properly. It will also get brighter as the dark gets denser."

"Good." Mrs Arnold strapped the helmet to her head, tucking her hair underneath it.

"There's a button above your head," said one of the men. "When you get to the bottom, press it." He closed the cage door and Malcolm turned on the motor. There was a long, vibrating hum as the cage descended down the well. Mrs Arnold took off her Armani sunglasses and pushed them into her backpack. She could see the men's heads looking down at her from the top of the well. She smiled: they looked like burst footballs.

It was a two hundred metre drop to the bottom. The air got cooler as the cage descended lower and lower. The hum of the motor died in the distance, leaving her in an eerie stillness. She was surprised to see insect life so far beneath the desert: the shaft wall was covered in ants, scurrying this way and that in an urgent hunt for food. She wondered what they could find to eat down here.

The cage hit the bottom of the well with a small thud. Mrs Arnold stepped out and looked around her. She was standing in a small tunnel, hewn out of the red granite by an underground river that had dried up hundreds, probably thousands, of years before. It snaked off into the darkness, twisting like a giant worm.

Mrs Arnold felt something under her feet. She looked down, the flashlight on her helmet swivelling to illuminate the smooth rock. There were bones scattered all over the place. Human bones. She saw a skull, its split cranium crawling with busy ants. She wondered if its owner had fallen down the well whilst trying to draw water.

The cage rattled slightly as someone at the top shook the rope impatiently. Mrs Arnold remembered the button. She stepped back inside the cage and pressed it. The cage bars started to vibrate slightly and the cage disappeared slowly up the well. Ten minutes later it reappeared, with a grinning Mr Ping inside it.

"Dry air in here," he said. "Means it has a good ventilation system. There's a big place round the corner. We are on the right track." He let himself out of the cage and consulted the map. "First we walk along the tunnel. It says here that it leads into the Cave of Decision."

He walked along briskly, closely followed by Mrs Arnold who was recording data on her Dictaphone. "We are approaching destination C. The time is 09.12, local time. The date is the 16th of July 1996. We should locate Object Gamma within the hour."

"We are here," said Mr Ping. The tunnel had led to another cave, an enormous round chamber full of surprisingly fresh air. "The round cave is like a hub of a bicycle wheel. There are entrances to six passages here. One leads to the desired crypt. One leads back to the exit. The other four lead to deadly traps. The map calls them tunnels of no return."

Mrs Arnold inspected the gaping entrances. They all looked exactly the same, black mouths waiting to devour someone.

"Perhaps we should call Malcolm and the

boys," suggested Mr Ping.

"No."

"You pay Malcolm good money," said Mr Ping. "Might as well use him."

"Malcolm and his men were not my idea," snapped Mrs Arnold. "The Bureau insisted I bring them along. Typical male chauvinism if you ask me. The powers that be figured a woman couldn't do the job properly without an Indiana Jones in tow."

"Okay," Mr Ping glared openly. "We'll find the right entrance. But there's no clue here on the map which is the right one."

Mrs Arnold studied the entrances again, her eyes taking in every minute detail.

"I think it's this one," said Mr Ping.

"Why?"

"Just a hunch."

"I think it's this one myself," said Mrs Arnold.

"What makes you say so?"

"Just a process of elimination," she replied. "It wouldn't be the one opposite the exit, that would be too obvious. So we're left with four tunnels, two to the right, two to the left. My guess is that it's one of the two on the left. The Arabs associate the left with evil. Most Bedouins consider it offensive to touch food with their left hand. Some refuse to walk on the left side of the street. They consider it bad luck."

"But which one is on the left?" asked Mr Ping. "There are two."

"The one furthest left, of course. Follow me,

Mr Ping." She started towards the tunnel. The archaeologist hesitated. "What if Mrs Arnold is wrong?"

"Then we get to die young and beautiful," snapped Mrs Arnold, her patience wearing thin. She hurried her step angrily, eager to get to destination C. Mr Ping, feeling humiliated, struggled to keep up with her. "The tunnel widens," he observed weakly.

"Good, we could do with a bit more fresh air."

"Perhaps the ground will open up, swallow us whole."

"For goodness sake, Mr Ping. I hired you because you are an eminent archaeologist. Don't turn into a superstitious fool on me."

"People who hide urns are most devious," said Mr Ping. "They set clever traps." Mrs Arnold stopped dead in her tracks. She spun round on her heels, her eyes blazing with fury. "How do you know about the urns? You never saw them."

Mr Ping couldn't quite hide a smug grin. "As you say, Dr Ping is an eminent archaeologist. He takes no time to figure out the truth."

"Mr Ping, this is a serious breach of your contract..."

"No worries," said Mr Ping. "I will tell no one."

"Alright then," she seemed to calm down at once. "Let's get the sucker." She ran along the tunnel, running her hand along the wall. As she had guessed, it led to a crypt: a small chamber with a very low ceiling. As befitting a shrine in a Muslim country, there were no statues decorating the walls, just panels of flowing, delicately sculptured script. There was a single grave in the centre: a simple marble box that had turned a dull brown with age.

"Do you know what the panels say?" she asked Mr Ping. The archaeologist studied one of them. "Here lies the father of all evil. Let them who come into this secret place allow his ashes to rest in peace. Let them who steal the sleep of the wicked take with them the curse of all mankind..."

"Gruesome twaddle," said Mrs Arnold. "Help me open the grave, Mr Ping." They lifted the heavy marble lid, wincing under the weight, and placed it against a wall. The grave was full of dead insects, mostly scorpions and scarab beetles with enormous feelers.

"I won't touch it," said Mr Ping.

"Suit yourself." She took a pair of leather gloves from her backpack and slipped them on. She plunged her hands into the sea of insects, feeling for the urn. "Here it is." She lifted it out with a flourish, insects cascading from its lid. Unlike the other three, age had not tarnished this urn at all. It sparkled in the glow of the flashlights, the angels in the red seals as clear as images on a film screen.

"It's beautiful," gasped the archaeologist.

"Yeah." Mrs Arnold put the urn in her backpack and drew out a gun. "You shouldn't have found out about the urns, Mr Ping." The colour drained out of the archaeologist's face. He started to tremble. "You cannot kill Mr Ping," he stammered, his voice choked with fear. "I will tell no one, absolutely no one."

"I cannot risk it," said Mrs Arnold. "My client requested absolute secrecy. He insisted on it." She pointed the gun at his heart and pulled the trigger.

Chapter 10

The woman behind the counter at Quik Prints sighed, flicking at a large bluebottle that was insisting on settling on her grey hair. "It's going to be a hot summer," she complained. "There are flies everywhere already."

Nicola handed her a blue receipt. "We've come to collect our photos."

The woman looked at the receipt closely. "Cotten," she said. She turned to a box and rifled through it. "A, B, C, Ca, Ce, Colby, Cotten. Here you are." She handed the photos to Nicola, smiling. "Pictures of your boyfriend?"

Lin Yu giggled. "In her dreams."

"They're pictures of Mark Dylan's house," said Nicola. "They're for a school project."

"I don't like that Mark Dylan," said the woman behind the counter. "All those strange clothes and bizarre make-up. I don't like men with make-up."

Nicola paid for the photos. "It's stage make-up," she defended Mark. "It's not the same as ordinary make-up."

The woman smiled again. "Still, I don't like it. It's a bad influence on the kids." She turned to serve another customer, an old lady who wanted a picture frame for her daughter. Nicola and Lin Yu left the shop.

"Let's see them," said Lin Yu.

Nicola opened the envelope. The pictures

had turned out better than she had hoped. Every single one of them was perfectly in focus. The ones taken in Mark's study were especially well-lit, as if they'd been taken by a professional photographer.

"Wait until Miss Harman sees them," said Lin Yu. "We're going to get a straight A for this project."

Nicola frowned. "What's this?" She was inspecting the picture of the three urns, the one she had taken at Lin Yu's insistence. She held it up for Lin Yu to see.

An ominous green face was hovering above the urns, its mouth open to show a pair of sharp, pointed fangs.

Miss Arnold sat in a chair, her expensive jewellery catching the light from the candles on Mark Dylan's mahogany desk.

"You have done me proud," said Mark, his fingers caressing the fourth urn.

Mrs Arnold smiled her well-rehearsed, professional smile. "Don't thank me, Mr Dylan. Thank the Bureau."

"I shall certainly recommend your organisation to my friends," said Mark. "I'm sure Michael Jackson might want you to hunt down something for him. Jacko likes collecting unusual artefacts."

"We would be more than happy to help Mr

Jackson." Mrs Arnold pulled a small red book from her bag and placed it on the table. "I believe you wanted this back."

"Ah yes, did you find it useful?"

"The Bureau couldn't have found the urns without it."

Mark opened the book. "I wonder if it's all true."

"What's true?"

"The legend in the book. You know, it says here that if I open all the four urns, Count Loris, the father of all vampires, will come back to life."

Mrs Arnold shrugged. "I prefer to believe in the power of my bank balance, Mr Dylan."

"Your bank balance," said Mark. "That reminds me." He reached for his cheque book and a pen. "How much do I owe you?"

"Two million dollars. Please make it payable to the Bureau."

"Right." Mark wrote out a cheque and handed it over. Mrs Arnold slipped it into her bag without looking at it. "Thank-you very much, Mr Dylan. It's been a pleasure working for you." She stood to leave.

"Thank-you Mrs Arnold. I'll show you to the door."

"I'll see myself out." She turned and walked out of the study without once looking back. Mark heard her shoes clattering on the marble floor. The front door opened and shut with a bang. A frightened owl hooted as a car engine started. Mark smiled and looked at the four urns.

It was time to find out the truth.

"It's a coincidence," said Nicola. She was sitting on Tim's bed while he examined the photograph of the green face floating above the urns.

"It looks like a vampire to me," said Lin Yu. "It's got pointed fangs."

"Don't be silly," said Nicola.

"Vampires do exist," insisted Lin Yu. "They are part of every culture in the world. The Malaysians believe in the pontianak, an undead spirit that hides in the branches of the banana tree. The Chinese have the P'o, a vampire that is meant to fly. Here in the West we laugh at such unexplained phenomena but that does not mean they don't exist. My grandfather was a policeman in Malaysia. He saw a pontianak once."

"I don't believe that for a second," said Nicola. "Everyone knows vampires are a figment of the imagination. Count Dracula was based on the life of Vlad the Impaler, a nasty baron with a taste for torturing people. But he wasn't a vampire at all - just a nutcase."

"I can't say I wholly believe in vampires," said Tim, "but I read somewhere that the ancient Assyrians believed in the Ekimmu, the restless spirit of a person who was not buried with all the right ceremonies. The Ekimmu wandered around the earth in search of food and drink. When desperate, he would suck people's blood."

Nicola looked unimpressed. "That was a long time ago. Even if vampires did exist back in time, modern science has wiped them all out."

"Some things don't change with time," said Lin Yu. "People still live and die."

"Alright," Nicola conceded. "But what has that got to do with the photograph? I don't think there's a vampire wandering around Mark Dylan's house."

"It's a pretty old house," Tim pointed out. "A lot of weird things must have gone on in there. And you've got to admit that Mark Dylan is a strange chap. You saw his collection of strange objects. What about those urns on the desk?"

"The strangeness is all an act," said Nicola. "It's something to keep the public interested between singles."

Lin Yu shook her head. "I think the urns have something to do with the vampire's face."

"Even if that were true," said Nicola, "what can we do about it? We can't very well march up to Mark's house and say, 'Hey, Mark, you've got a vampire hovering over your desk.' "

"No, we can't," agreed Tim. His computer bleeped, indicating he had just received E-mail. "It's probably that pathetic Internet addict again." He clicked the mouse button and a short message appeared on the screen, the words flashing on and off like a danger signal:

DANGER GROWS BIGGER EVERY DAY. HELP.

"I'm getting tired of this," said Tim. "I'm switching off."

Lin Yu came close to the screen. "No, answer it."

"What?"

"Answer the message."

"What shall I say?"

"Ask the sender who he or she is."

"Alright." Tim sat down and keyed in the question: Who are you?

The screen went blank for a second. Then the answer came, the letters quivering with urgency:

VAMPIRUS.

Chapter 11

Mark locked the windows in his study and drew the curtains. It was a warm night but he wanted to feel secure. The urns stood on his desk, bathed in candlelight.

Mark sat in his chair and looked at them for a long time. "It's time to find out the truth," he said to himself. "Do vampires really exist? I shall soon know."

He picked up a penknife and started whittling away at the sealing wax on one of the urns. It was tedious work - the wax had hardened over the years - but he persevered.

Without warning, the lid fell off the urn and rolled across the flagstones, coming to a halt under a sideboard. Mark ignored it. He tipped the urn over and grey ashes poured out of it into a silver dish. He grinned to himself. At least one part of the legend was true. He opened the second urn. More ashes. He opened the third and the fourth. The silver dish was overflowing now. He stirred the ashes around with a letter opener, humming one of his own tunes. He was disappointed. No Count Loris had appeared. The legend wasn't true after all. Two million dollars for a pile of ashes I could have scraped out of my own barbecue, he thought.

A foul smell reached his nostrils. He looked up to see a ripple travelling across the surface of the ashes. His heart missed a beat. Perhaps the legend was true after all. These were the ashes of the infamous Count Loris.

The ripple grew bigger. The ashes started flying about, forming a little whirlwind. Mark moved closer, to have a better look. Something hurled a handful of ashes in his face. He coughed and closed his eyes to rub them. The bad smell grew stronger, making him want to throw up. There was a hiss, followed by an evil-sounding snigger. Mark opened his eyes. The dish was empty. Not one single fragment of ash remained. He heard the snigger again and looked up.

A six-foot man was standing behind his desk. He had small, mean eyes, the whites flecked with red specks. His skin was a dirty white, mapped with thousands of blue veins. "Good evening," he said. Mark could see that he had sharp, yellow fangs.

"Good evening," he replied. "Are you Count Loris?"

The vampire chuckled, his eyes bright with mischief and hatred. He raised his powerful arms, showing off long, dagger-like nails.

"I am Mark Dylan," said Mark. "I am a musician." He gestured at the urns. "I set you free."

The vampire smiled. "Thank-you. You deserve a reward for this, little man." He reached out and grabbed Mark by the throat. Mark tried to struggle but he was no match for the Ancient One. The Vampire pulled him close to his face. His fangs sank in his neck.

Ruha stood in the rain, looking up at Lin Yu's window. She had made contact at last, she had found three people who could help her get the urns back. All four urns were now in the same house. The danger was bigger than ever.

For a while now Ruha had been contacting the mortals through their speaking machine. Now she needed to make physical contact. She had to speak to them, to explain everything. But before she could do that, they had to invite her into one of their homes. She couldn't visit anyone unless they invited her in.

Lin Yu lay still in her bed. It was raining. She could hear the rain pattering against the bedroom window. A car passed by outside, filling her room with orange light, making the knick-knacks on the windowsill cast long shadows on the carpet. The hallway clock ticked loudly, emphasizing the silence in the rest of the house.

A storm was building up. A distant flash of lightning filled the room with bright, neon-white light. The faint rumble of thunder followed. Lin Yu looked at the clock on her bedside table. It was five minutes to midnight. The witching hour.

She thought back on the events of the day: the horrid green face in Nicola's photograph, the message on Tim's computer. Was a vampire really trying to make contact with them? Was there someone who needed help? When she was little, Lin Yu had believed in gnomes and fairies. She had thrown pennies into wishing wells and made solemn wishes. Her grandmother still believed in all sorts of charms and spirits. On New Year's eve she would clean the house with a new broom and give all her friends and relatives lucky money to attract wealth and prosperity. But somewhere along the way Lin Yu had lost her belief. At school she swore that she believed in ghosts and monsters. But only because it made her stand out from the crowd. Deep inside she wasn't so sure. Now she was all confused. Could her grandma be right after all? Could the other world, the world only glimpsed in fantasy books and films, really exist?

Another bright flash of lightning made Lin Yu jump. For a moment all the colours in the room seemed to jump out at her, then everything was plunged into darkness. The storm had reached Erlington.

Lin Yu got out of bed to close the curtains. Yet another bolt of lightning split the sky, showing up cracks in the clouds. Lin Yu screamed: there was a face at the window, a pale, drawn face full of pain and sorrow.

78

Chapter 12

The Vampire, the Ancient One, looked at the prostrate body lying on the floor. He grinned evilly. It was good to have a disguise, to look young and fashionable again.

The Ancient One adjusted his collar. He couldn't look in the mirror - there would be nothing of this finery to see in the looking glass - but he knew he looked good. His host lived in a manor; he was obviously rich and powerful. His clothes would, no doubt, be of the finest quality. They fitted perfectly.

The vampire dragged the body across the room and locked it in a Victorian coffin. Smiling, he wiped his hands on a silk handkerchief he had found in his back pocket. He returned to the desk and sat down.

There was a picture of his host on the front cover of a magazine. He was a bit on the thin side. His face had been handsome once but now wrinkles had started to appear around the eyes. They were cleverly hidden with make-up but the Ancient One wasn't fooled. He needed nourishment. He needed blood.

The Count chuckled. It wasn't going to be difficult impersonating the famous singer. The desk was groaning under the weight of Mark Dylan biographies.

Nicola sipped her tea slowly, holding the mug with both hands. "You alright, sweetheart?" Her mum stroked her hair, smiling the way she always smiled when she wanted to comfort her only daughter.

"It was such a horrible nightmare," said Nicola. "I've never had nightmares before."

"It's over now, sweetheart." Mum put the cup on the bedside cabinet, next to the alarm clock Nicola had had since her seventh birthday. "Do you want to tell me about it?"

"I was walking on the downs," Nicola began. "All alone. I met this girl with a pale face. She was my height, only thinner. Her hair was all white. Her skin too. It looked sort of bleached. There were little blue veins all over her face, like a spiders web, only the strands were all crooked and broken."

"It must have been a vivid dream," Mum said.

Nicola pulled the duvet up to her chin. "I saw her while she was still far away. Her white robe stood out against the dark sky. It seemed to glow, like the full moon. The girl didn't walk. She sort of glided across the grass, coming towards me with open arms. I tried to run away but I was rooted to the spot. My feet were sinking in a patch of quicksand that had suddenly appeared beneath me. I was in it right up to my ankles. The girl came closer and closer, ducking under the trees - that's when I saw her face clearly. By the time she reached me, I was fighting for my life. I kicked with my feet to stay afloat and called out to her but the patch became a pit. She looked over the edge at me. I held out my arm but she wouldn't take it."

"'It's you who should be helping me,' she said. 'I am the one who needs help.'"

"I screamed at her then. She burst into a rage, pounding the earth with her fists. 'It's all in vain,' she cried. 'We are all lost. The Ancient One has come.'"

Mum looked at Nicola in horror. "This one's for the books alright," she said. "Why don't you come and sleep in my bed?"

"There's one last bit," said Nicola. "I reached out and grabbed the girl's hand. It came away in mine and I drowned in the quicksand, taking her pale hand with me."

The Ancient One opened the study window and flew out. He soared towards the dark sky, drinking in the smell of the raging storm. The rain spattered on his clothes but left him curiously dry. He opened his arms wide, as if to embrace the village that lay underneath him.

I am back, he said to himself triumphantly. The fools could not keep me away forever. I am back.

He turned on his back and changed himself into a bat, then a fly. Even after all these years he had not forgotten the intricate process of change. He settled for a moment on a web, pretending to be trapped. A spider scuttled out of its hiding hole, eyes blinking expectantly. He waited until it was close enough to touch him then changed into a bat, tearing the web with his crooked wings. The spider, alarmed, leapt to the ground. He lunged after it, caught it and popped it into his mouth to suck its blood. Once he had finished, he spat its chewed carcass out onto the grass.

Oh, it was good to be awake again.

He flew high up in the air, winging through the rain clouds, daring the lightning to singe his wings. When he tired of horseplay, he willed himself back to his original shape and drifted on the air currents.

He saw a man lying on the street below him. He was dozing, his chin resting on his lap. Even from his height, the Ancient One could smell the cheap alcohol on his breath. He was a vagrant.

Things hadn't changed that much in two hundred years.

The Ancient One grinned to himself. I think it's suppertime. He crossed his arms and dropped down next to the sleeping man.

"It's your lucky night," he said.

Chapter 13

"It's the girl in my dream." said Nicola. "She had the same skin, the same white hair."

"I saw her very clearly," said Lin Yu. "She was obviously in pain."

Tim handed round a plate of chocolate biscuits. "She must be the same person who is trying to contact us through the Internet."

"Why don't we try contacting her?" said Nicola. "She must be somewhere close if she has appeared at Lin Yu's window."

"Great." Tim turned to his computer. "What shall I ask?"

"Ask her who she is," suggested Lin Yu.

Tim typed in a question: Are you there?

The answer came back right away: Yes. My name is Ruha Slavinka.

Tim asked a second question: What do you want from us?

Help.

"She's got to be a bit more specific than that," said Nicola.

How can we help you? typed in Tim.

Ask me in, came back the reply. I can only come in if you ask me into your house.

Tim hesitated for a second. Then he typed in an invitation: Come in, Ruha Slavinka. You're welcome in my house.

She appeared shortly afterwards, a small white bat that fluttered in through the open window. She hovered in the air, uncertain where to settle down. The three of them instinctively looked away, embarrassed. "Close your eyes, please. I am not used to mortals looking at me." They obeyed. "You can look now." They opened their eyes: a thin girl was sitting on the edge of the bed, her white hands folded neatly on her lap, like a baby girl at school. She dropped on the bed.

"Welcome to Erlington," said Lin Yu.

"Thank-you. I have been in your village for a few nights now. I met a farmer on the outskirts and he invited me in."

Ruha didn't open her mouth but they could hear her voice in their heads. It sounded hollow and faint, as if she was speaking to them through a very long tube. "But thank you for accepting me into your house. I have not been inside a house for nearly two hundred years."

"How can we help you?" asked Lin Yu. Now that she was looking at Ruha, she didn't feel at all confused. She wasn't scared either. All she could feel was pity - a great pity for this miserable girl who was doomed to wander an alien world long after her time had come and gone.

"There is great evil afoot in your village," said Ruha. "The Ancient One has come back."

"The Ancient One?"

Ruha nodded at Tim. "He is living in the big manor on the hill, preparing to take over the village and then the country."

"Who is he?" asked Nicola who, like Lin Yu, felt sad for this forlorn little girl.

"His name is Count Loris. He is one of the seven Ancient Vampires who came to Earth after the great fall."

"The great fall?"

Ruha smiled ruefully. "When Lucifer and his angels rebelled against God, they were thrown into Hell. But seven of them chose to become vampires. The Earth was still young then. No mortals had yet emerged from the wilderness. The vampires waited and practised their talents. They learnt how to change shape. They became birds and insects, and slimy creatures that inhabited the murky waters of the emerging seas. Their minds learnt how to communicate without the use of speech. Telepathy, I think they called it. But there were obstacles they never managed to overcome. The Sun, God's most dazzling creation, had an adverse effect on them. It melted their bodies. Silver too was an enemy. They could not touch it, nor could they approach something decorated with it. Worst of all, they found that they could not cry. They felt pain and anguish but they could not find release in tears. That was their biggest curse. It's still the same for vampires everywhere.

"When man appeared, they preyed on him. They caused wars and plagues. They delighted in annihilating God's greatest handiwork. In Ancient Rome, they influenced Nero, who burnt his city and killed thousands of people. During the dark ages, they ruled supreme. Havoc was wreaked on the Earth. Terror ruled. But one by one the Ancients were destroyed. They grew fat and foolish. Mortals got wise to their games and pursued them relentlessly. Soon there was only Count Loris left. He had always been the clever one, the leader. For centuries he dodged the silver spears and the holy waters of the vampire hunters, travelling from one end of the world to the other to create mischief. He was a judge during the Spanish Inquisition, a witch burner in the villages of England.

"Then in the early years of the 19th century, Count Loris was caught by a famous Greek vampire hunter. He was lured into a silver coffin and drowned in the Aegean Sea. For one hundred years, the world knew peace. Then some divers hunting for sunken pirate ships discovered the coffin and opened it. Count Loris awoke and unleashed his anger on the world. The result was the First World War. After that he grew weary of grand gestures. His power started to wane. It might have been the fact that people were starting to discover the science behind the superstitions. Count Loris, who had always thrived on fear, found there was less and less of it around in the big, bustling cities he liked. He was forced to retire to small mountain villages, to rural communities where people still believed in the evil eye and the magic charm. My Rumanian village of Ari Lasov was such a place: a small farming community where boys grew up to tend sheep and girls married and raised children.

"Count Loris came to visit us late one afternoon. I was sitting by myself on the edge of the village, looking after Grandpa's goats. It was hot and I fell asleep. The sun had slipped behind the mountains and I still dozed on, lulled by the heady perfume of the meadow flowers. He woke me up.

'Excuse me,' he said. 'Can I come in?'

'Of course you can come in,' I said. 'This meadow belongs to no one in particular. Anyone can come and sit here.'

'I can't come in unless I'm invited,' he said. 'It's one of my principles.'

I laughed at his odd joke. 'You must be a stranger. Welcome to Ari Lasov.'

He stepped into the meadow then, grinning from ear to ear. He was such a handsome man, tall and neat, with clean hands and fashionable clothes, the likes of which I had never seen before. I think he must have put a spell on me.

'I am Count Loris,' he said. I don't remember much else of that first encounter. He sat beside me and all of a sudden there was a pain in my neck. The waning colours of the meadow seemed to regain their brightness, as if the sun had come back up from behind the mountains. The shapes of the flowers around me ran into one another. Some time later my father found me lying on the grass, my clothes wet with dew. I was delirious with fever. There was no sign of the Count. I told my daddy about him but he would not believe me. 'You must have dreamt him,' he said. 'No one like that has been seen in the village.'

"But it soon became clear what I had welcomed into our midst. I got weaker and weaker until one night my heart stopped beating altogether. The Ancient One had drained me of blood and so I became a vampire. I walked around the village at night, feeling lost and bewildered. One by one, the children in our school fell ill and died too. Their parents buried them in the little cemetery behind the church but they would not stay put. They were seen to wander the streets at night, crying out piteously. The villagers blamed me for the tragedy that had befallen Ari Lasov. I was forced to go into hiding. Meanwhile the Count became bolder in his misdeeds. He stole geese and chickens. He attacked old women on their way to church before sunrise.

"The village was up in arms. They hunted him down and pierced his heart with a sharpened stake. They buried his body beyond the village boundaries. That night I had the strangest dreams. The Count's history was revealed to me. I travelled with him through time, learning of his horrible doings. He also revealed his true self to me and I saw for the first time the powdery white skin, blemished with blue veins and the dull, red eyes.

"The next night the Count came back to life. The ritual had not worked. He visited the sick in our local alms house, feeding off the infirm. He fed on more animals too. The shepherds lost their livelihood. Cows were found drained of blood. Dogs went missing.

"The villagers, more enraged than ever, hunted him down again. This time they found his coffin hidden under the crypt of the local church. They set it alight. When his body was burned, they scattered the ashes in the hills, praying and chanting.

"But again, their efforts failed them. With sheer force of will, the Count brought all his ashes back together. He awoke once again, more fierce than ever. It was then that we turned to the monks who lived above Ari Lasov. Their abbot drew up a plan for us. Count Loris was once again trapped - this time in the attic of a blind ninety year old spinster who believed she had rats in the house - and bound inside his coffin while he slept. He was burnt before sundown. His ashes were then divided into four piles and sealed in silver urns. Each urn was hidden in a different part of the world. Thus his ashes were prevented from ever coming together again and giving him life once more.

"I, as the culprit who had welcomed the beast into our village, was chosen to be his guardian. I accepted my role without hesitation. Guilt lay heavy on my heart. I wanted to make amends. I travelled with one of the urns to China. I was sealed in a coffin and laid to rest in a crypt close to the chapel where the Count's ashes were interred. That way I could guard them in my sleep. Even as I drifted off, I knew that I would wake soon after the ashes were touched.

"That happened a few months ago. A Chinese farmer broke into the crypt and stole the urn. He sold it to an antique dealer in Shanghai. By unfortunate coincidence the dealer had also acquired the abbot's red journal and the maps he had drawn. The urn and the book were sold to Mark Dylan who found the other urns. Now Count Loris is on the verge of coming back, if he has not returned already."

Ruha opened a golden locket hanging on a chain round her neck. "This is a picture of Count Loris. When he died, the colours all but disappeared. Now they are bright as the day they were painted. The Count is close."

Silence hung over the room. "What can we do?" said Nicola at last.

The vampire spoke softly. "You must go to Mark's house and bring me the urns. I shall hide them in new places."

Chapter 14

Alfred Gary parked his Ferrari Testarossa in Mark's driveway and crossed the patio towards the front door. The outside lights were off, making it difficult to see in the pouring rain. "Not my lucky night, tonight," Alfred said to himself. He rang the doorbell and Mark himself answered the door. Alfred thought he looked pale and drawn. His eyes were all red, as if he'd been smoking in a closed room. "You alright, Mark?" he said.

Mark grinned broadly. "Never felt better. Come in, Alfred. I've got some plans I want to discuss."

"Plans? Mark, it's three o'clock in the morning. I thought you were in some kind of trouble. You didn't drag me all the way here to discuss some foolish plan, did you? The wife's terribly upset."

Mark turned on him with alarming ferocity. "I pay you good money to be my manager. I can jolly well summon you when I like."

"Summon? Mark, what are you on about? I'm not your slave, you know. You were nothing when I discovered you playing drums at the *Spike and Kettle*. You'd still be gigging in pubs if it weren't for me."

"I would have been discovered by someone else," said Mark, opening the door to the study. "Now let's get on with the meeting so you can return to your darling wife as soon as possible."

He settled behind the desk, the reading lamp turned away from his face. "I've been looking at the schedule for the next tour," he said. "I want to cancel the afternoon appearance at that charity benefit in March."

Alfred's mouth dropped open. "But Mark, you promised the organisers you'd headline months ago. You were first on the list. You know Guns 'n' Roses will come over from the States to do it if you don't. Where will that leave us?"

"I don't want to do it," Mark insisted. He held up his hands. "End of argument."

Alfred sighed. "I'll have a talk with the organisers, then. But don't blame me if the tabloids crucify you. This is one of Princess Di's favourite charities."

Mark did not reply. He looked through his notes. "This television appearance on a Saturday morning children's programme," he said. "Cancel it too. I don't look good on Saturday mornings."

Alfred did not argue. "I don't know why you wanted to do that in the first place. I reckoned you fancied the presenter, the girl with the big lips."

Mark ignored that last remark. "We don't have enough tour dates in Eastern Europe. I want to do Rumania. And Poland."

"You hate Eastern Europe," said Alfred, not quite believing his ears. "You always say the kids there don't have enough money for merchandise. What's come over you?"

"I have unfinished business in Rumania,"

said Mark.

"I beg your pardon?"

"I think it's a growth area. Those countries are going to be rich soon. We must get in on the act before the others. I bet you Guns 'n' Roses will be playing there soon."

"Alright."

"That's it, then." Mark stood up. "Can I get you a cocktail?"

"Mark, you've never had a cocktail in your life."

"A beer, then."

"Nah, Sandra'll be up, waiting for me. I should have called her, really. Told her you were alright. She was worried about you."

"Give her my regards," said Mark. He showed Alfred to the door.

"Your patio lights don't work," said the manager.

"I know. I'll get someone to fix them." He closed the door quickly, before Alfred could say goodnight. Fumbling in the dark, the manager got into his car and turned on the ignition. A crow squawked suddenly, startling him out of his wits. "Blow me down with a feather," he muttered. The enormous bird had settled on the bonnet of his car. It glared at him with rheumy yellow eyes. "Shoo," Alfred said. The crow flapped its wings but stayed put.

"Shoo."

Alfred got out of the car and waved at the bird angrily. The crow hopped on to the roof of the Ferrari, scratching the paintwork with its enormous claws. "Get off," he said angrily. He picked up a pebble and threw it at the bird, hitting it on the beak. The bird shrieked loudly - a shriek that sounded more human than bird-like - and hopped back down on the bonnet. Alfred could smell alcohol on its breath, as if it had been drinking. "Stupid nuisance," he muttered. He pushed the bird off the car with his bare hands and got back in.

The crow watched him drive away standing on the gravel, its head cocked to one side. Its eyes looked a bit like Mark Dylan's.

Ruha held her hands to the moon and climbed higher into the clouds, her robe flapping around her legs. She breathed in the cool night air, revelling in the scent of the cut grass and budding honeysuckle. Flying was one of the only joys that came with being a vampire. Everything else was awful and horrid, like a never-ending nightmare from which you couldn't hope to wake.

There was the hunger, for instance. It was gnawing at her insides, twisting round and round, a whirlwind that could only be subjugated by blood.

Ruha refused to drink human blood. Her grandfather had taught her to drink the sap of trees. It satisfied her hunger for a while, it numbed the whirlwind. But it tasted awful. The thought of her grandfather made her think of her childhood. Where were her parents and relatives buried, she wondered? What did Ari Lasov look like today? Was it still a remote mountain village, the home of simple farmers and shepherds, or had it expanded into a bustling town, full of strange machines and modern inventions?

A soft, red light beneath the thin clouds caught Ruha's attention. She let herself fall, hurtling towards it. It was a bedroom lamp, framed by a window with chintzy curtains. Ruha peeped in. A little girl was lying on a bed, wrapped in a thick, brightly patterned duvet. Her father sat in a chair, reading stories from a book in a funny, squeaky voice. The girl was laughing, clapping at the jokes.

The scene saddened Ruha. It was her punishment, she realised, to look in on life without being able to take part in it. As a child she had always wondered what marvels lay beyond the mountains around Ari Lasov. She had heard about distant countries; she had dreamed of travelling the world, making friends and meeting people. Now all that was a distant memory. For who would befriend a vampire? Who would want to share their life with someone they considered evil and dangerous? She floated away from the window, like a snail retreating into its protective shell. To cheer herself up she thought about Tim and Nicola and Lin Yu. They were friends of sorts, even though they were afraid of her. She had heard their quickened heartbeats while she had told them her story. She had noticed the way they kept to the other side of the room, as far away from her as possible.

And who could blame them?

At least they were going to help. Tomorrow they were going into the strange manor on the hill to retrieve the missing urns. Then Ruha could return to her coffin, where blessed sleep would blot out this eternal pain.

A crowing cock reminded Ruha that dawn was approaching. She had to find somewhere safe where she could sleep away the day. Casting her eyes to the ground, she saw a farm. There was a barn behind it. It looked warm and dry. Ruha folded her arms and plunged to the ground, stopping only when her bare feet were ten centimetres above the grass.

The barn looked inviting, full of hay and old lamps covered in cobwebs. A cow sat in a corner, chewing dried grass. "Just my kind of place," Ruha said, only half-joking. She found an old seaman's chest behind a pile of broken furniture. Even after all these years she could smell a faint trace of salt in the wood, mixed in with the aroma of old tobacco. Quickly, she climbed in and closed the lid above her.

Outside, the cock crowed again. The sun came up.

Chapter 15

Harry Palmer, owner of the Fourwinds Farm on the edge of Erlington, sat on the edge of his chair, grunting as he pulled on his old wellies.

"D'ye fancy another cup of coffee afore ye goes?" asked Mildred, his wife of the last fifty years.

"Nah, I'll have some with me breakfast when I get back, pet." Harry stood up, rubbing his aching knees with his gnarled hands. It was getting more and more difficult to get up at the crack of dawn every day. *Once I could jump out of bed at two in the morning,* thought Harry ruefully. *No problem. I could get out there and start milkin' the cows afore the sun'd show his face o'er the downs. Now all I can think of is lying under me comfy blankets, wigglin' me old toes.*

"I'll make some nice porridge," said Mildred. "It'll be nice an' warm when ye get back."

"Ta." Harry went out in the back yard, closing the kitchen door quietly behind him. When the children were young he'd always made sure he didn't wake them up by banging the door. Now the children were all grown up and living in big cities. The eldest was a teacher in Birmingham. The second was out in Australia, doing something or other in the tractor business. And the youngest, the baby, had left them young. Harry tried not to think about his youngest daughter. She had liked summer mornings like this, all cool and drizzly with summer rain. "God is watering our garden, isn't he, tata?" she would say. She had always called him tata, even when she had hit eighteen and went to work for a building society down in Erlington.

Harry let himself into the hen coop, treading softly in the straw. The hens' heads twitching backwards and forwards fussed around him. "Here y'are, here y'are," he cooed softly. He scooped meal out of his jacket pocket and scattered it on the ground. The hens clucked contentedly, pecking at the food with their dirty beaks.

"Nice hens," said Harry. He rifled through the nests and lifted half a dozen eggs. They felt warm against his skin, full of life and health. The hens watched him put them in a square wicker basket, lining them up neatly in a row.

"Ta, me beauties." He left the coop, making sure the latch was secure. The sun was up now, stretching and yawning beyond the low hills of the downs. Harry stopped to breathe in the morning air. It looked like it was going to be a good day, warm but clear. He tightened his hold on the egg basket and hurried past the barn towards his allotment. He never went in the barn now; he hadn't set foot in there since his bank manager had forced him to sell the sheep. Molly the cow still lived there but Mildred milked her now, usually in the evening. Harry preferred to spend his time on the allotments behind his farm, checking on the marrows and the zinnias. If his friend Gerry was there, force-feeding his precious rhubarb with liquid feed, they would sit on upturned buckets and talk about the good old days. Harry and Gerry liked a good natter, especially if it reminded them of better times when they were younger and healthier.

A strange buzz reached Harry's ears. He frowned, trying to guess what was causing it. No one around kept bees as far as he knew, not even the odd young couple who'd moved down from London to live 'in harmony with Mother Earth'. Could a swarm have escaped from Saltham, fifty miles to the east? Harry had read in the *Erlington Leader* that someone over there had started a bee farm, making honey to sell in health shops around Sussex. Perhaps that's what the noise was.

The buzz got louder and angrier. Harry put a step on it, almost tripping over his own feet in his haste to get to the allotments. He saw a dark red cloud hovering above his sunflowers, the ones he'd taken a chance on and planted early so Mildred could take part in a local flower competition. It was bees alright, thousands of them.

Harry took a step backwards. All the bees he'd seen before had been black, with a tinge of yellow. These monsters were red, a dark angry blood-red. Other bees, Harry knew, flew in harmony, connected to each other by swarm instinct. But these bees were behaving most oddly. Each one seemed to be buzzing erratically, flying independently of its brothers and sisters. Harry's mind reeled. Should he stand still and hope the bees would ignore him, or should he run away as fast he could, praying his movements wouldn't attract their attention?

A faint cry reached his ears. At first he thought it was a puppy, frightened by the bees. Then someone called his name. "Harry."

It was his friend, Gerry.

"Ger, where are you?"

"Harry. Over here."

He dropped the eggs on the grass, panicking. The voice was coming from his friend's allotment, behind the sunflowers. "Harry." Shaking, he tiptoed round the edge of the allotment, keeping away from the swarm. He moved slowly, like a sponge diver treading the ocean floor. The swarm hummed furiously, a machine out of control. He worked his way round his vegetable patch, past the early zinnias and the onions. Gerry was lying on the ground, completely covered in bees. All Harry could see of him were his bright green eyes, staring out, wild with fear.

"Don't move a muscle, mate," he whispered. "I'll get help."

☠

"Aunt Grace says Mark's going back to London tomorrow," said Tim. He was leaning against the kitchen cupboards talking to Nicola on the phone. "So we can go to his house and get the urns."

"Ruha will be pleased," said Nicola.

Auntie Grace came into the kitchen, carrying a bag of groceries.

"I have to go," said Tim. He hung the phone on its cradle. "Want a cup of tea, Auntie Grace?"

Auntie Grace nodded, putting the bag on the table. "Gerry Collier's had the most dreadful fright," she said.

"What sort?"

"He's been attacked by bees. Old Harry Palmer found him. He was lying on the ground in his allotment, completely covered with buzzing insects. Just thinking about it makes my skin crawl."

"Is he in hospital?" asked Tim.

"He's being treated for shock. Strange thing is, when the police arrived there was no sign of the bees. They'd disappeared into thin air. Only Gerry and Harry saw them."

"Perhaps they imagined it all," said Tim, filling the kettle.

"No, I've just been talking to Lucy Collier. She said the nurses in the emergency room at the hospital said Gerry's blood pressure was sky high when they brought him in. The man had had his blood pressure checked only a couple of days before. It was normal. No, he'd had a big fright all right."

"Perhaps the bees are hiding somewhere, then," said Tim, "waiting to attack someone else."

"Don't you go around putting scary ideas in people's heads," Auntie Grace admonished him. "The village is already buzzing as it is."

"They must be somewhere," said Tim.

"Yeah," said Auntie Grace. "The weird thing is no bee farmer has reported a runaway swarm. And both Gerry and Harry Palmer say that the bees were red in colour, as if their wings had been dipped in blood. No one has ever seen blood-red bees before."

"Weird." Tim poured hot water into a teapot. "Would you like some toast?"

"No thanks," said Auntie Grace. "I've got to go over to my sister in a second. She's having a new carpet laid and she wants some help moving old bits of furniture into the barn. I'll come back at two and make you some tea."

102

Chapter 16

The night had pounced on the day, swallowing up all its light. Auntie Grace put the phone down and sighed. "It's Mark," she said. "He wants me to go up to the manor right now. He wants something to eat."

"It's half past ten at night," said Tim. "Can't he make himself a sandwich?"

"Mark can't even boil an egg properly. But he's never asked me to go up there this late in the day, not unless he's had dinner guests or people sleeping over for breakfast meetings. And he usually gives me a day's notice when he wants anything like that." She took her coat off the peg and put it on. "I hope he's alright. He sounded a bit odd."

"Odd?"

"His voice was a bit weak, like he's got a cold or something. Perhaps all he needs is a hot toddy."

Tim frowned. "Ring him up and tell him to open a tin of baked beans."

"I can't," said Auntie Grace. "It's no bother, really."

"Lazy idiot. Shall I come with you?"

"No, love, you know how he hates people coming up to the house. I'll be back soon. You do some homework or watch some telly. There's a good film on tonight. A Grace Kelly weepie."

"But what about the bees?" said Tim. "It's not safe to be out on your own on a night like this."

"I'm not getting out of the car until I get to the house," said Auntie Grace, rifling through her handbag for the car keys. "I'll be alright."

"I'll write a letter to Mum, then." Tim settled back in his chair, his elbows resting on the kitchen table.

"You do that," said Auntie Grace. "And don't answer the door while I'm away."

"I won't."

"Bye then." She closed the back door behind her and ran through the summer drizzle towards her car. Stupid rain, she thought, why do we have to have rain even in summer? She got into the car, turned on the ignition and eased it up Bolton Lane. There was no one about, not even people having barbecues in their back gardens. They must have been driven indoors by the bees, thought Aunt Grace.

Something hit her windscreen with a soft thud and was instantly brushed away by the windscreen wiper. It left an arc of dark goo, like a black rainbow, on her windscreen.

Heaven help us, thought Auntie Grace. What could that have been? The wiper erased the arc, like a teacher wiping a badly written sentence from the blackboard. Auntie Grace concentrated on turning up Lincoln Pass, a narrow lane often used by motorbike riders coming home from Brighton.

Another object hit her car. This one landed on the bonnet and stayed there. It was followed by another and another. Sighing, Auntie Grace got out of the car to have a look. The things on her car were frogs, small frogs. Even in the dark she could see that they were bright green, with dark spots that reminded her of malignant moles. Auntie Grace suppressed a shudder. Gritting her teeth, she went back to the car and put on a pair of gloves. Then she flicked the slimy creatures off her car, one by one. They left patches of sticky blood behind them. Or perhaps it was mud; she really couldn't tell which.

A dog howled in the distance, a long, drawn out howl that suggested the animal was caught in a trap. This time Auntie Grace couldn't suppress her shudder. What in the name of creation is going on, tonight? she thought.

She peeled off the wet gloves and thrust them in her coat pocket. The wind felt cold on her hands, more like a winter chill than a summer breeze. She got back into the car and turned the key in the ignition. The engine wheezed, like an old man with 'flu.

"Great," said Auntie Grace. She turned the key again impatiently, pressing the accelerator as hard as she could. Another wheeze, then silence.

The trapped dog howled again. It sounded nearer this time, as if it was just round the corner on Harry Palmer's farm where Auntie Grace bought her free range eggs for Mark Dylan.

Perhaps the creature is not trapped at all, thought Aunt Grace with a shiver. Perhaps it's rabid and on the loose. Perhaps it's heading this way...

Count Loris looked at his watch. It was almost midnight. The housekeeper was late. An hour late. The Count drummed his fingers on the desk impatiently. He wanted a feed, and he was curious to find out what the woman looked like. Had household staff become so liberated in the two hundred years he had been missing that they dared ignore their master's wishes? No, something must have happened to the woman. He picked up the phone, then put it down again. The last thing he wanted to do was to alert her stupid family. There was no need for that, not when he could find out what was happening himself.

Count Loris went upstairs and opened a bedroom window. He stood on the sill, feeling the summer breeze on his face. What could he turn into tonight? He was tired of bats. And he hated flies - they were so dirty and insignificant. Ah yes, he would be something regal tonight, something that befitted his position as the Most Ancient One.

The Count closed his eyes and concentrated hard. His skin turned black; thick velvety fur sprouted on his arms and face. Mark's eyes, usually a mottled green, turned a bright, incandescent yellow. The pupils narrowed into slits, sharp as daggers.

Roaring with delight, he leapt from the window, hitting the ground with well-padded paws. A dozen birds in the trees rose in panic, filling the night with their screeching. He was a black panther, a powerful animal built to tear its enemies apart.

He charged down the driveway and through the gate. Small creatures bolted from his path, their ears pinned back to their heads with terror. He felt great, all-powerful.

He saw the housekeeper's car ten minutes later. It was sitting in the middle of the road. The housekeeper was inside it, obviously waiting for help. He could smell her. It was the same smell she left in Mark's house, sweaty and earthy. He deliberated on what he should do. Should he tear her apart with panther teeth? Or should he reveal his ancient form, hypnotising her with his eyes so he could relish her blood for nights to come? He could drain her of blood in a week and then she would be a vampire too. She would be his servant forever.

Silently, he approached the vehicle. There were dead frogs on the road, alien creatures that normally inhabited the rainforests of South America. He chuckled. Mother Nature could feel him coming. She was quaking in her boots, malfunctioning. The housekeeper sensed his presence. "Hello...is anyone there?"

He leapt into the branches of a tree and purred, keeping his voice as low as possible.

"Pussy?" The woman smiled, obviously delighted. Her head poked out of the open window, her eyes scanning the dark for a glimpse of him. Mortals liked animals, he remembered, especially the stupid domesticated kind. He purred again. "Pussycat?" His purr turned to a snigger, a cruel laugh. The smile vanished from the housekeeper's face. She sat back in her car, her hand on the door. "Who's that?"

With a fierce roar, he leapt out of the tree, landing on the roof of the car. The woman screamed; her hands flew to her ears. He stepped down on the bonnet and turned to face her, yellow eyes blazing. "Raaaa."

She screamed again and, sobbing, wound up the window. He snarled, showing her his pointed fangs. Her fists hammered the glass.

"You shall perish," he said, sending the message straight into her mind.

Then a bright yellow vehicle came round the bend in the road, a light flashing on its roof. Count Loris glared angrily. He slipped off the car, slinking nimbly into the bushes from where he could watch unobserved.

"Are you alright, ma'am?" Men ambled out of the yellow truck. The housekeeper burst into tears. "There's a panther on the loose," she sobbed. "It leapt on my car."

The men started at the bush, fear rising in their masculine throats. The Count could feel their trembling; they could not hide their cowardice from him. He toyed with the idea of showing himself, just to see how fast they would run back to their truck. But he decided not to. Let the woman rant and rave. No one would believe her. She would see the disbelief in their eyes, mingled with pity. It would drive her insane.

He stretched his paws and turned into a bat. It was time for a feed. He would settle scores with the housekeeper some other night.

After all, she would be coming to the house every day.

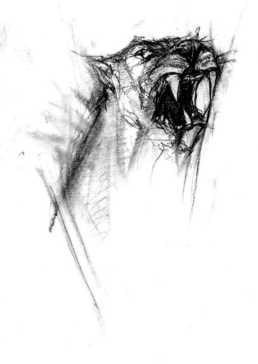

Chapter 17

Tim found the address to the Strange Phenomena Society's Internet site and keyed it into his computer. It took only a short while for his server to download the information into his machine. Tim clicked the mouse button, searching.

There it was: the Vampire Section, written by an American writer called Henry Newman. Tim scanned the text, reading quickly. There was a good deal of information about real vampires. Most of it was eyewitness accounts told to the author by different people, usually farmers from rural communities, nearly all of them in Eastern Europe. He selected a first person account by a Polish shepherd and read through it.

"Legend had it that our village of Karvosa had been haunted by a powerful vampire once," the shepherd had written. "Now we suspected that he was back. Many of our sheep had gone missing. A few had been found, drained of blood and tossed in ditches. There were other signs too. Nature was in revolt, as if it was trying to warn us. A plague of ants marched on our wheat fields, destroying the crops. Locusts rained from the skies, only to disappear a few days later. Strange animals roamed the countryside, filling the night with their howls and our hearts with fear. It seems that a vampire's arrival is always heralded with strange signs of nature..."

☠

Count Loris flitted through the sky on his bat wings, his ever-seeing eyes searching for a mortal. He spied a little barn tucked away behind a farm. Did farmhands still sleep in barns, he wondered? Or had they all grown rich and bought houses and proper beds like their masters?

He dipped his right wing and flew down in a curve. Another bat joined him, its wings beating frantically to keep up with him. He hissed and the bat flew away, frightened. The barn door was locked. So was the tiny window next to it. He flew round the side and found a large crack. It was too small for a bat to fly through, but a fly would have no problem...

He flew in and settled on a bale of hay. Rotten hay. There was a cow tied up in the corner. It was fast asleep, its tail flicking lazily at imaginary flies. The Count's attention was drawn to the other side of the room. There was a pile of old furniture there: an old dresser, a heavy chest of drawers with a missing leg, a collection of old fishing rods, a seaman's chest. Its dented metal lock glared at him like an accusing eye.

The Count stiffened, instantly taking human form. There was someone in the chest, someone whose heart did not beat like a mortal's. The Count closed his eyes, to see through the wood. It was the girl: his first victim from Ari Lasov. So the little wretch had followed him here. The fools had chosen her to be his keeper. But what could a little girl do against his might? He was the Most Ancient One. Time had taught him all its tricks. She was barely two hundred years old and she had probably spent most of those lying in a coffin, close to his ashes.

He would destroy her. Break her in two like a dry twig. Opening his eyes, the Count advanced towards the chest. The girl was fast asleep, exhausted by the lack of blood in her veins.

A mouse squeaked in the dark. The Count frowned. He could not get any closer to the girl. Something was pushing him back. His eyes scanned the chest again. Yes, she had blessed olive leaves stitched into the hem of her dress. Whoever had chosen her as guardian of the ashes had done his homework well.

The Count snorted angrily. The fools would not get him once more. He could not destroy the girl yet - not until he could get a mortal to remove the olive leaves from her garb. But he could make her life a misery. He could stop her from getting to him.

The Count leapt into the hay and grabbed a rat by the scruff of its neck. It was a large creature, the size of a mature squirrel. The Count held it up to his face, looking deeply into its mottled eyes. It squealed, frightened, clawing the air with its sharp nails. "Ssshhh..." The Count stroked its back. "Ssshhh." A glazed look came to its eyes. Its tail fell limp, swinging like a pendulum. He whispered gently into its ear and set it down on the floor.

The rat scurried to the chest. One hop and it was sitting on the lid. It reached out with one claw, feeling for the lock.

"Go on," the Count urged it on.

The rat lowered its head and grabbed the key in its powerful teeth. Its head swivelled round. There was a grating noise as the key turned in the lock. The Count chuckled. The silly girl was locked in. There was no way she could get out when she woke up, not even if she turned herself into a mite. There were no holes in the chest she could crawl through. It had been designed to keep out the smallest drop of water.

The sun came up over the downs, lighting up the mist. Lin Yu stood at her window, looking out at the countryside. The window was open to let in the fresh air. Today's the day, she thought. Mark Dylan goes back to London in the afternoon. We can retrieve the urns for Ruha.

She wondered where the vampire was. Was she sleeping in a grave somewhere? Or had she found shelter in a deserted farm?

The phone rang in the kitchen, making Lin Yu jump. Her mum answered it, jabbering in Malaysian. "Alright." Mum placed the receiver on the kitchen table and came to the bottom of the stairs. "Lin," she called. "Are you awake? Nan wants to have a word with you."

Lin Yu skipped downstairs in her nightgown. She picked up the receiver "Nan. Where are you?"

"I'm staying with your Auntie Mei in Kuala Lumpur," Nan's voice sounded distant, unclear. "The baby's due any day now. Lin, are you alright?"

"Of course I am," said Lin Yu. "What makes you ask?"

"I had a dream about you," said Nan. "One of my special dreams. That's why I rang. Lin, be careful. I think my dreams are telling me you are in danger."

Lin Yu swallowed hard. Nan's special dreams were usually accurate, like the weather forecast on the radio. "I'll be alright," she said. "I'm not doing anything dangerous."

"I haven't told any of this to your mother," continued Nan. "There's no need to involve her in any of this. I know how she panics. But in my dreams, you were fighting a red monster. He had teeth as big as elephants' tusks. Lin, I don't know what you are up to out there. But I have some advice for you: Take..." Crackling on the line drowned out Granny's next words.

"I can't hear you," shouted Lin Yu.

"Place..." said Granny. "Desk.....it's very.....important."

"I can't understand a word you're saying,"

Lin Yu shouted. Mum came over. She took the phone from Lin Yu. "Mum...?"

There was only silence. The line had gone dead.

☠

Ruha woke up. She had overslept. And for the first time since becoming a vampire she had had a dream. A terrible dream. She couldn't remember any of it now, but she was still scared.

Ruha lifted her hands to open the chest. The lid wouldn't budge. She pushed again. Nothing. Someone had locked her in.

Trying not to panic, she closed her eyes and peered through the lid. The key had turned in the lock. She was trapped.

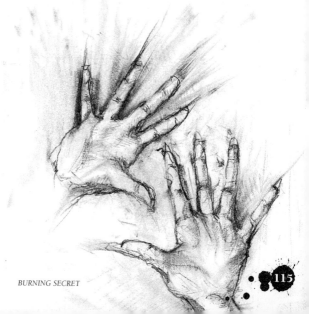

Chapter 18

"I'm coming with you," said Tim. He kicked off his bedroom slippers and put on his shoes.

"Great," said Auntie Grace. "That panther frightened me silly yesterday. I don't know if I can even drive, I'm so nervous."

Tim put his arm around her.

Auntie Grace hunted around the kitchen for her car keys. "You don't believe me either, do you, Tim? I don't blame you, really."

"There's a lot of weird things happening," said Tim. "Raining frogs, blood-red bees. What's so strange about a black panther roaming the streets of Erlington?"

"It's the hole in the ozone layer," said Auntie Grace. "It's changing the weather and the animal world is going crazy. Perhaps that panther came to England aboard a yacht or something. There's a marina over in Hastings. People go to all sorts of foreign places in their boats nowadays."

The phone rang and Tim answered it. "It's Nicola," he said. "She wants to come over to Mark's house."

"Not tonight," said Auntie Grace. "I can't handle kids running around the place tonight, not after all I've been through last night. We're only staying an hour or so. I just want to change the sheets in the master bedroom and bring some laundry home for tomorrow. Mark always leaves the bedroom in an absolute mess when he's recording. I suppose his mind is on his music."

Tim looked disappointed. "I think we should let the girls come. Safety in numbers and all that. We didn't misbehave last time."

"I suppose not."

Tim smiled and spoke into the phone before Auntie Grace could change her mind. "Nicola, ring Lin Yu. Meet us outside your house in half an hour. We'll give you a lift."

☠

Auntie Grace parked the car in Mark's driveway. "He still hasn't fixed the lights," she complained. "I'll get old Vic from the electrical shop to have a look at them tomorrow."

"Don't worry," said Nicola. "It's not quite dark yet. We can see our way around."

She unfastened her seat belt and got out of the car, followed by Tim and Lin Yu. It had just stopped raining and the grass was wet. "Wipe your feet before you come in," warned Auntie Grace. She unlocked the door and let them in. "Don't touch anything, will you?"

"We're just taking some more photos of Mark's study," said Lin Yu. "Nothing else."

"Alright." Auntie Grace hurried into the kitchen and donned an apron. Mark had left the remains of a cooked breakfast on the draining board: baked beans and grilled bacon. "Funny,"

she thought. "Mark's a longtime vegetarian."
She swept the food into a bin and put the plate
in the sink. The rubbish bag was full, so she tied
it up and took it out to the plastic bin in the
back yard.

Night had fallen. Auntie Grace peered
around her, half expecting a black panther to
leap out at her from behind the bins. A cat
miaowed in the bushes, making her skin crawl.
She dropped the bag and ran back indoors.

"Hello, Grace." It was Mark, wearing his
trademark Raybans.

"I thought you were up in London," she said.

The singer smiled - not the famous smile that
had captivated fans since the early 1980's, but a
horrible, false smile that gave Auntie Grace the
shivers. "I've got a present for you."

"What kind of present?" She sounded
suspicious. This wasn't like Mark at all.

He removed his glasses to reveal yellow,
jaguar eyes. Before she could scream, he leapt
across the room, grabbing her by the arms. "An
everlasting one." He laughed, a manic laugh
that echoed in her ears. His lips curled back,
exposing long, pointed fangs.

"Say hello to eternity," he said.

☠

Ruha beat against the lid of the chest with
her fists. It was no use. Her hands were getting
bruised and the wood had not splintered one

single bit. Her mind reeled. She had to get out. Night had fallen. The mortal children had gone up to the house. She had to be there, to protect them, in case the Ancient One had come back.

The barn door creaked as someone opened it. Ruha heard the shuffling of feet.

"Mollie...?"

The cow in the corner mooed and stamped her foot. A bucket was set down on the ground. "Here ye are, old girl. Here's something good to nibble on." It was a woman's voice, kind and gentle.

Ruha hammered her fists on the chest, drawing blood. "Help," she called. "Help."

The woman ignored her. "'Tis getting too warm to stay indoors all night, me Mollie," she said. "I'll get Henry to move ye out. I know he don't come to see ye anymore, but this thing wiv the bees has med him think a lot."

The cow mooed, nuzzling the woman's arm. The woman laughed and picked up the bucket. "What's that ye're sayin' pet? Speak up, you know I'm as deaf as a doorpost nowadays."

Chapter 19

Tim looked at the things on Mark's desk. "The urns are gone," he said.

"Mark's put them away somewhere," said Lin Yu. "They could be anywhere." Nicola looked around the room.

"The collection," said Tim. He crossed the room, turning on the overhead lights. Nicola and Lin Yu followed.

"They might be in the coffin," said Nicola.

"They're too precious to be tossed into a coffin," said Tim. "What about that cupboard?" He pointed to a display cabinet.

"Let's have a look." Nicola turned the key. "Yes, here they are."

She opened the cabinet and pulled out an urn. "Oh no," she gasped. "It's been opened."

Ruha lay still, every follicle in her body alert. The deaf woman picked up her bucket, humming to herself out of key. Ruha closed her eyes and concentrated all her mental energies. If she couldn't talk to the mortal, then she could speak directly to her mind.

"Come here, dear lady," she thought. "Put your bucket on the floor and come here."

The cow, sensing Ruha's thought projections, mooed nervously, flicking her tail. The old woman stopped humming. "What is it, Mollie?" she said. "Them summer flies bothering ye?"

"Come here," Ruha commanded. "Approach."

The old woman put the bucket down. "I must be going senile, Mollie," she said, "I just remembered Harry's old sea chest. Do you remember Harry's old sea chest, Mollie? I haven't thought about it in a long, long time."

☠

Auntie Grace opened her eyes. She was sitting in the big armchair in the living room. How did I get here? she wondered. She remembered being bitten on the neck by something. But what? Mosquitoes? A gnat? Auntie Grace's brain was all fuzzy; she couldn't remember a thing. She went to the hallway and looked in a mirror. There were two puncture wounds on the left side of her neck. "Bees," said Auntie Grace.

She went upstairs to fetch some medication. "Tim? Nicola?" A faint sound was coming from one of the guest suites on the ground floor. It sounded like a running tap. Auntie Grace let herself into the bathroom and pulled the light cord. A tap had indeed been turned on; water was swirling around in the basin. She turned it off. Behind her a medicine chest swung open. She turned round and screamed: the chest was full of crawling maggots.

☠

"They're all open," said Nicola. "What shall we do now?"

"You will do nothing." The three of them spun round on their heels. Mark had just come into the room, wearing his shades.

"Good evening, sir," said Tim politely. "I'm Grace's nephew. Auntie said we could look around. We're doing a summer project about you."

"And what are you going to concentrate on: those urns?"

"We're not going to write about the urns," Nicola replied. "We're going to take them away. Mark, you're in danger."

"Am I?" Mark laughed, showing surprisingly large teeth. "And why is that?"

"Don't you know the legend?" said Lin Yu. "The vampire will come back if you open the urns."

Mark glared. "And how do you know that? Who told you about it?"

"No one told us," Tim cut in. "We found the pigskin folder on your desk. I'm afraid we read the journal."

"It's all superstitious rubbish," said Mark. He marched over to the display cabinet and pulled out a biscuit tin. "The ashes are still here, look. The vampire has not returned."

Chapter 20

Mrs Palmer ran her fingers round the edges of the sea chest. "I remember when me old 'arry brought it home, Mollie," she said. "Course, he wasn't old then. We called him young 'arry. He brought the sea chest over to me mum's and dumped it at me feet. 'There,' he said, 'that'll convince ye I'm not goin' back to sea, not ever.' He put 'is compass in it and his old uniform. And when we took over the farm, we brought it wiv us, so 'arry could remember his days at sea. Course, the ole compass is still in here. I expect the moths have had the uniform for their tea, though."

She turned the rusted key and pushed back the lid. A white moth flew out of the chest, its wings beating frantically.

Mark put the lid back on the biscuit tin. "You see," he said. "The world is still safe after all."

"But..." said Nicola.

Lin Yu, suspecting her friend was going to mention Ruha, butted in. "How did you get the urns, Mr Dylan?"

"I bought them," replied the singer. "Now if you'll excuse me..." He pushed the shades up his nose.

"You have some interesting things in here,"

Lin Yu said quickly. "That painting on the wall, for instance. That's Victorian, isn't it?"

"Correct. It's called The Laughter of The Sorrows," he said. "The Victorians had a morbid fascination with death. There are all sorts of hidden messages in this picture."

"I like this," said Lin Yu, picking up a silver tray from the display cabinet. "What period is it?"

Mark glared at her. "I have no idea. Put it down, please. That's worth a lot of money. I must be getting back to work."

"There are some words etched in the tray," said Lin Yu. "I think they're in Latin. What do they mean?" She held out the tray for Mark to see.

"Get back," hissed the singer. "Don't you dare bring that thing close to my face."

Ruha flew towards the strange house, her white hair flying around her face like a cloud. She had to get the urns. She had to bury them as quickly as possible.

Reaching the house, she settled on a tree in the garden. Lights shone from several windows. She wished she could go inside to help the mortals but she knew she couldn't. Mark Dylan had to invite her in himself.

"You have no reflection," said Lin Yu, holding

up the silver tray. "You are Count Loris."

Mark glared angrily. "You meddling fools." His voice deepened as his lips contorted and changed shape. His skin broke out in running sores, his face seemed to melt, the features running into each other like hot wax.

"Ugh," said Nicola.

A foul stench of rotting bodies permeated the room. Mark disappeared completely, and Count Loris stood in his place, his marble-white skin pulsating with blue veins. "Prepare to meet thy maker," he cried. He lunged forward, hands outstretched. The children screamed and scattered, all three of them running in different directions.

Chapter 21

Auntie Grace screamed. The maggots were crawling out of the medicine chest towards her, leaving trails of thick, putrid slime behind them. She backed away.

There was a slithering noise in the bath. A long finger was emerging out of the plughole, its flesh turned a dull blue with cold. Auntie Grace stood rooted to the spot, unable to lift a foot. The blue finger beckoned, getting longer all the time. It reached out and tapped her on the shoulder. A manic laugh came out of the plughole, echoing around the porcelain bath.

"Say hello to eternity..."

The finger wrapped itself round her neck like a noose, pulling her towards the bath. "Come and see what's on the dark side..."

"No," Auntie Grace wrapped her trembling hands around the finger. "No."

The finger released its hold and she fell backwards, bumping her head on the bathroom door. Quickly she reached out to turn the handle. But the door was locked. Someone or something had locked it.

The voice in the bath sniggered. Auntie Grace fainted.

☠

Tim ran out of the study and down the corridor. Fear had made him light-headed. He couldn't think. He tried calling out for Auntie Grace but no sound came out of his mouth.

Count Loris came charging after him. Tim could feel his cape snapping at his feet, like a dog waiting to bite. A terrible howl filled his ears. The Count turned into a bat, flitting above his head, teasing him. Tim stopped and grabbed a chair. He hit out blindly, yelling. The bat turned figures of eight, dodging the chair. It danced in the air, revelling in its power. Tim hit out again. This time he was successful. There was a loud slapping noise. The bat fell to the floor, motionless. Tim dropped the chair. He approached the creature cautiously, his eyes fixed on its little head. He poked it gently with his toe. No movement. Could he have knocked it senseless, perhaps killed it? He bent to pick it up, his hand trembling uncontrollably.

The bat twitched suddenly and leapt up. It fastened its teeth on his hand. Tim screamed. The bat turned into Count Loris, bellowing with rage. His eyes were red with rage, the pupils dilated to pinpricks. "You," he said, tightening his hand around Tim's throat, "are dead meat."

✠

Nicola burst into a bedroom. She had to find a phone. She had to call the police. Her fingers found a switch and she pressed it. Blinding neon light filled the room, dazzling her. She spied a white phone on a table by a bed. She hurried over and dialled 999. "Hello," she cried. "This is an emergency."

A voice answered her plea through a symphony, crackling. "Speak up, please. We have a very bad connection. I can't hear you."

"This is an emergency," shouted Nicola. The line went suddenly clear. A peal of laughter filled her ears. "Nicola," whispered a new voice in the receiver. "The bogeyman is coming to get you. Say hello to eternity."

Nicola dropped the phone and crawled under the bed.

✠

Tim kicked the vampire in the leg and he relinquished his hold on his throat. The boy backed down the corridor towards the study. The vampire followed, sniggering, his hands reaching out, long, curled nails swaying hypnotically.

"You think you can destroy me?" he hissed. "I am the Ancient One. I was ruling the earth long before your puny little civilisations had even been conceived. I am supreme. I shall turn you into a vampire and then you shall wander the earth as my unwilling assistant."

"Stay away from me," said Tim.

"I can feel your creative juices flowing," said Loris. "You think you want to destroy me. But what you really want is to be a part of me and my infinite world of possibilities."

"No, I don't."

"Imagine it, child. The power to live forever. The power to go wherever you please, to see the sights you have always wanted to see. I can give you the time to achieve all that your greedy little heart desires."

Tim reached the study and backed through the door. "I'd like to do it my way," he said.

"Your way?" The vampire laughed. "You are running out of time, child. Even now, your feeble mortal body is waiting to let you down. You shall age as you struggle to achieve your dreams." He turned the palm of his hand upwards in invitation. "Come to my side, boy. You are not like the rest. You yearn to be a famous writer, an eminent scientist, an explorer. With me, you can do all those things."

"I don't think I want to live forever," Tim said. He felt the edge of Mark's desk poking his back.

"You do," said the vampire. "Don't you want to go to the moon? Or the stars? Don't you want to meet people from other planets? It's only a matter of time."

"Is it?" Tim reached behind him and grabbed two rulers from the desk. He whipped them round and held them in Loris' face like a cross.

"Fool," snarled the vampire. "I have survived three visits to the gas chamber and one death on the electric chair. Do you think a primitive hangman's noose is going to scare me?"

Ruha's heart skipped a beat. Something was amiss; she could feel it. She flew to a window and looked in. Count Loris had cornered Tim in a study. There was no way the boy could escape. She could feel his panic emanating in waves towards her.

He was lost. She had to help him. Ruha closed her eyes and studied the objects on the desk. Her mind fastened in on one of them, a shining silver compass.

Lin Yu opened the front door and ran out into the garden. Where was Ruha? Why didn't she come and help them?

Something reached out of the ground and grabbed her ankles. She screamed and started tugging at her foot. The thing pulled harder, dragging her down. Lin Yu heard a faint rustling in the grass, something scuttled over her shoe: a spider.

Lin Yu looked around her in alarm. The lawn was crawling with eight legged monsters. They were marching towards her, their eyes glinting like diamonds in the moonlight, their little mouths open in anticipation.

"Ruha," she called feebly. "Ruha, where are you?"

Count Loris held up his hand towards a window. "Listen," he said. "Nature is in revolt against man. Maggots and worms rise up against you. Spiders plot to annihilate you. The mortals have destroyed this planet. But you, boy, are different. You can save yourself. Come with me. I represent the new order. You and I can conquer the world, bend the rules as we please. We decide who dies and who lives. We shall have absolute power over life itself."

"I don't want to be like you," Tim said. "I don't want to be a monster, not even if I can live forever."

"Very well, then." The smile vanished from the vampire's face, giving way to a hideous glare. "You shall perish like all the rest." He opened his mouth and hissed. His teeth grew longer, sharper, like swords emerging from their sheaths. The veins on his face widened, spreading like a pulsating map across his skin.

"Please," said Tim. "We mean you no harm."

The vampire laughed, ignoring his plea. "You shall be the first. Already the others are surrounded by my minions. By sunrise, you shall be nothing more than brainless fools." He advanced, hands held out before him, the curled nails straightening out into daggers.

Tim inched his way along the desk. He was trapped. There was no way he could run past the vampire out of the study. He racked his brains. What could he do? Crosses were useless against this monster. He had to think of something else.

The vampire came closer, stench pouring out of his mouth. "Please," Tim whimpered. "Please." The vampire let him run behind the desk, a lion toying with a captured mouse.

"Do not be afraid," the Count sniggered. "It's only a little bite, a minor wound. Such a small price to pay for an eternity of power."

"No." Something in Tim's brain made him look down at the desk. His eyes searched frantically, trying to locate a weapon. He saw the compass, lying on a sheet of graph paper. "Throw it." A voice - Ruha's voice - whispered in his head. "Silver is lethal to him. It's your last chance."

He raised his hand and threw the weapon at the Count, aiming at his heart. The vampire ducked but, caught unawares, he wasn't quick enough. The compass embedded itself in his shoulder, staining his cape with blood. A terrible shriek escaped from his mouth. The silver burnt a hole in his flesh, releasing blue smoke. He stumbled backwards across the room, his arms flailing wildly. "You shall perish for this, you imbecile," he screamed. He tried to pull the compass but already the silver had spread in his veins, sapping him of energy. He fell backwards into the fire, the flames licking at his cape. The fire engulfed him at once.

Chapter 22

Auntie Grace woke up. Why was she lying on the bathroom floor, her clothes soaked with sweat? I must have slipped, she thought. Bumped my head on the floor. She felt her head. No pain. No bumps.

She looked up at the medicine chest. It was open. Small bottles were lined up neatly inside it, waiting to be used.

Perhaps she had come in here to fetch some medicine, then? But for what? She had never felt better in all her life. Auntie Grace stood up and washed her face with cold water.

Tim watched in horror as the vampire crawled out of the fire and across the flagstones. His face was melting; bones were showing through the burning flesh. "Water," he begged. "Give me water."

"No," said Tim firmly. The vampire stood up, tottering on his burning feet. He held up his arms in supplication, his long nails curling in the intense heat of the flames. "Please."

Tim hesitated. It seemed monstrous to let a creature, even an evil one like this, perish in such pain. Then Ruha's voice spoke in his head again: "Stay." The vampire fell to his knees. "Curse you," he said. "You shall not be rid of me. I shall come back to wreak my revenge on you and your children. I shall be back." Those last words died in his throat. A moment later his mouth curled and ran down his neck. He fell on his face, immobile.

Lin Yu stared at the ground. The spiders had disappeared. The thing that had been holding her down had relinquished its hold. She bolted across the lawn towards the house.

"Tim," she called. "Nicola. Where are you?"

Tim watched helplessly as the burning corpse turned to ashes. He knelt on the floor and poked it gingerly with his finger. "Strange, how things work out," he thought.

A faint, knocking sound made him look up. "Someone, help, I'm suffocating in here." Tim turned his head, trying to locate the voice.

"It's Mark Dylan. I'm in the coffin." He ran across the room and released the singer. "Thanks," said Mark. "I thought I'd been trapped in one of my own videos there." He felt his neck with his hands. The puncture wounds were gone. He was safe.

Auntie Grace hurried in, Nicola in tow. "What is going on here?"

"It's a long story," said Tim.

"Yeah," agreed Mark. "As long as history itself."

Auntie Grace glared at the ashes on the floor. "What's all this? I hope you're not expecting me to clean it up tonight, Mark Dylan. I'm shattered."

"I'll clean it up myself," said Mark.

"Alright," Auntie Grace yawned. "We'd better get a move on, it's late. Where's Lin Yu?"

"I'm here," Lin Yu came into the study. Mark turned to Auntie Grace. "Make us breakfast, will you, love? I'm famished."

"Breakfast?" Auntie Grace shook her head angrily. "At this time of night? You must be joking."

"I'll pay you overtime," said Mark.

Auntie Grace smiled. "In that case, my lad, what you need is a good dinner."

"Alright," said Mark. "That'll be lentil bake for five, then."

Auntie Grace went to the kitchen to start making the meal. Mark put his hand around Tim's shoulder. "I want to thank you for saving my life."

"Don't thank me," said Tim. "I didn't save you. Ruha did."

Mark looked around the room. "You mean there's another nosy fan running wild around this place?"

"She isn't a fan," said Tim. "And she's not in your house. She can't come in unless you invite her."

"Alright," said Mark. "Let's ask her in."

Chapter 23

Ruha sealed the last of the four urns and placed it alongside the others on Mark's desk. "Take a good look at them," she said. "No one will ever see those four urns together again."

"Where are you going to hide them?" asked Nicola.

"I don't know yet," said Ruha. "But I am going to think up four new hiding places, really clever ones. And there are going to be no maps this time, no charts anyone can follow."

"That's good," said Lin Yu. "No one will ever be able to find them."

"And if someone does stumble on one," added Mark, "they will never be able to put two and two together, if you'll pardon the expression."

Ruha laughed, the first time in nearly two hundred years. "The evil Count Loris has said goodbye to eternity forever."

"Hear, hear!" said Mark. He shook Ruha's hand. "I have been foolish. I have dabbled in things I did not understand. As a result I put a lot of people's lives at risk. I am sorry."

"We all do foolish things," said Ruha. "I am no less to blame for all this than you are."

The others could see a cloud of sadness pass across her eyes. "If you ever get lonely," said Mark, "you can always come to see us. My door is always open to you. You are part of my family now."

"Are you sure?" Ruha felt choked with emotion. She had not heard a kind word for so long. She could hardly believe her ears.

"This is a big house," said Mark. "I've got state of the art security. You will be safe here. I can get you your own coffin. You can see Tim and the girls whenever you like..."

"We could teach you everything you need to know about modern life," Tim said. "There are lots of exciting things in the modern world: computers, the Internet, books and tapes and CDs."

"And you could teach us about your world," said Nicola "There is such a lot we can learn from the past. Stay, Ruha."

Lin Yu put an arm around her shoulder. "We are your friends. We accept you for what you are. Say yes to Mark. Accept our friendship."

"Alright, I accept," She wanted to say more but her voice caught in her throat. Something wet welled in her eyes. Trembling, she turned away from her new friends and let the tear run down her face.

BURNING SECRET

Part 3

2213

A fierce summer sun blazed out of a blue sky, making the newly trimmed supalawns in the Highfield International Stadium turn from a harsh green to a cool, refreshing blue.

"When's the ceremony gonna start, Miss?" asked a boy in a shiny white suit.

"Pretty soon, I should imagine," replied the teacher, a middle-aged woman with short hair and round, rimless spectacles.

The boy sighed and sat back in his seat. He was thirsty. He rubbed his hand over his shirt and the porous material secreted perfumed water into his pores, satisfying his thirst through his skin. Relaxed, the boy closed his eyes. His classmates watched the grass as the sun slid behind a grey cloud and the supalawns turned a contrasting, cheery yellow.

On the podium, a man walked on to an aluminium lectern and tapped his shirt pocket twice. Instantly, the five thousand people did the same.

"We are connected," said the man.

"Connected to life, liberty and the freedom of movement," chorused back the audience. They could not hear the man speak but his voice was relayed to them via ultrasound mini-microphones in their shirt pockets.

"My name is Gerry Saturn," said the man. "I am chief spokesperson for the European Educational Space Programme."

"May the power of positive thought be with you and the European Educational Space Programme," the audience replied.

Gerry smiled and performed a salutation with his right hand. The movement incorporated greetings from the twenty two approved faiths around the world. The audience responded with a minute of silence in honour of dead astronauts and space explorers.

"We are gathered here," said Gerry Saturn after the minute's silence had elapsed, "to launch the Space Time Capsule Programme." He pointed to a large silver cylinder behind him. "Hundreds of everyday objects have been collected by students around Europe to send to outer space. Our time capsule will orbit the far reaches of our galaxy in the hope that, one day, alien life forms will learn about the way of life on Planet Earth. The objects placed in the time capsule include CD-ROMS; videos, writing tools, food substitutes, thought waves captured on laser disc and 1000-bit holograms depicting a typical day in Earth school, certainly the best school in our solar system."

The audience burst into applause. Gerry acknowledged the appreciation by holding up his hand, palm towards the audience, fingers extended. Then he tapped on his shirt pocket, asking for immediate silence. He got it. A woman in a Peace Patrol uniform came on stage, carrying a small black box. She whispered in Gerry's ear, smiling.

"Citizens of Europe," said the spokesperson. "I am proud to tell you that Grade 1 citizen Ruha Slavinka, the main sponsor of the Space Time Capsule Programme has just joined us to witness the launch."

The announcement made the audience gasp in unison. Ruha Slavinka was a legendary figure in the world of Joyknowledge and Infotainment. She had come out of nowhere to found a publishing empire in the last years of the twentieth century. Since then her company had gone from strength to strength. It had branches all over the world, supplying whole countries with thought lasers and holographic entertainments. But Ruha herself was rarely seen in public. Afflicted with a rare and incurable skin disease, she found sunlight harmful and worked only at night. On important occasions she ventured out in a transport unit with blackened windows. No one ever saw her face.

"Citizen Slavinka has requested we put one last object in the time capsule," said Gerry. The woman held up the black box. "It is a mystery object and Citizen Slavinka has requested that we keep its contents a secret." She passed the box to Gerry who placed it in the time capsule and locked the shiny metal door.

"Citizens," he said. "It is time for the countdown." The audience clapped their approval as the time capsule was wheeled offstage and transferred to a space rocket precisely twenty kilometres away from the stadium. From the interior of her darkened transport unit, Ruha listened intently. The children were counting, their voices high with excitement. "Madam," the driver handed her a pair of vision enhancers. She strapped them to her eyes, searching the skies beyond the blackened glass.

A loud blast drowned out the children's voices. A cloud of smoke rose in the air, mushrooming over the stadium. Ruha watched the rocket soar above the skyscrapers, a silver needle against the deep blue of the sky.

"It is done," she whispered. "I am free of guilt at last. Goodbye Count Loris. You and I shall never meet again."

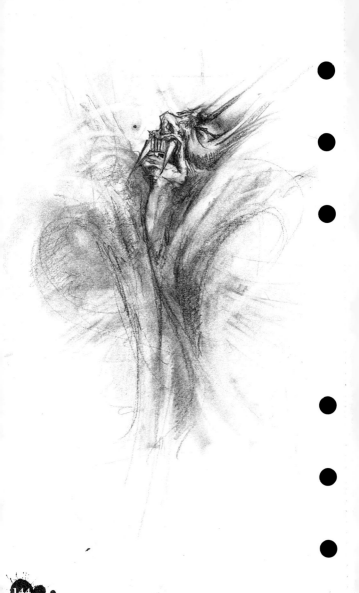

144